Aimee Bender is the author of the *New York Times* bestseller *The Particular Sadness of Lemon Cake* and of the collections *The Girl in the Flammable Skirt* and *Willful Creatures*. Her work has been widely anthologised and has been translated into ten languages. She lives in Los Angeles.

Read more about Aimee Bender and her work at: www.flammableskirt.com.

ALSO BY AIMEE BENDER

An Invisible Sign of My Own

AIMEE BENDER

 WINDMILL BOOKS

Published by Windmill Books 2012

2 4 6 8 10 9 7 5 3

First published in the United States in 2000 by Doubleday,
a division of Random House, Inc., New York

First published in Great Britain in 2000 by Review,
an imprint of Headline Book Publishing

First published in paperback in Great Britain in 2001 by Headline Review

Windmill Books
The Random House Group Limited
20 Vauxhall Bridge Road, London SW1V 2SA

Addresses for companies within The Random House Group Limited can be found at:
www.randomhouse.co.uk/offices.htm

The Random House Group Limited Reg. No. 954009

www.randomhouse.co.uk

A CIP catalogue record for this book is available from the British Library

ISBN 9780099558521

The Random House Group Limited supports The Forest Stewardship Council
(FSC®), the leading international forest certification organisation. Our books
carrying the FSC label are printed on FSC® certified paper. FSC is the only forest
certification scheme endorsed by the leading environmental organisations,
including Greenpeace. Our paper procurement policy can be found at:
www.randomhouse.co.uk/environment

Book design by Jennifer Ann Daddio

Printed and bound by CPI Group (UK) Ltd, Croydon, CR0 4YY

for suzanne and karen

Numbers are friends for me, more or less.
It doesn't mean the same to you, does it—3,844?
For you it's just a three and an eight
and a four and a four.
But I say, "Hi! 62 squared."

—MATHEMATICIAN WIM KLEIN

An Invisible Sign of My Own

Prologue

So.

There was this kingdom once where everybody lived forever. They'd discovered the secret of eternal life, and because of that, there were no cemeteries, no hospitals, no funeral parlors, no books in the bookstore about death and grieving. Instead, the bookstore was full of pamphlets about how to be a righteous citizen without fear of an afterlife.

The problem was that because of this life spurt, the kingdom was very crowded. The women kept having more and more babies, and the babies had no place to sleep because of the fourteen great-great-grandmothers and great-great-grandfathers that were crowding up all the bedrooms. All the old people were getting older and older, and there was no respect for elders because the elders were just like the youngers; there wasn't really a whole lot of difference anymore. Space was the real problem. So the king, getting crowded out of his own castle by the endless royal lineage, issued a decree. "Everybody in my kingdom," he said, "please pick one person in your family to die. I'm sorry, but that's the way it goes. If you don't want to do it, please leave. We will have a mass execution on Friday, and it will bring forth much more space and everyone will forever honor those who gave up for the cause."

So on Friday, the town congregated. A few folks had packed up their bags and left, but most stayed on the land they loved. The remaining families had spent the week choosing their offering. This wasn't as hard as might be expected; to be forever honored was appealing, and plus there was an unspoken curiosity in the town about dying—it was sort of like going on a trip to an exotic place no one had ever been before, and just having to stay there for good.

So that afternoon, each family that showed up in the town square had chosen one martyr to die for the cause of greater community space. There was a lot of weeping and praising going on, and finally everyone pushed forward a volunteer; that is, all except one family. This family simply could not pick. First the mother had said she would die, and then everyone in the family protested, and then the father said he would die, and everyone protested, and then the daughter said she would, and no one liked that idea, and the son offered, but that was no good either, and then the baby cried and they thought it meant she would, but she was the baby and that didn't make much sense at all. The whole family was arguing and crying and volunteering and pushing and shoving and finally the mother moved forward and said to the king's executioner: "We cannot pick, so we would all like to die together."

"Well, that's ridiculous," said the town executioner. "Then there will be none of you left. That spoils the whole point."

The rest of the town was irritated as well. They didn't want the whole family gone. This family ran the bakery and was particularly adept at making a fine sausage roll, with ground-up meat and nutmeg inside, so delicious it tasted like dessert.

The family took off to the sidelines to discuss. The rest of the families waved tearfully at their martyred volunteer, who each waved back, hands shaking with goodwill and terror. Finally, the difficult family stepped forward.

"Well," said the father, "how about this. We would like to offer a piece of each of us. With all these pieces combined, it will be as if one less person lived in town."

The town executioner cocked his head. "Continue," he said, interested. The mother stood forward, and said, "You may have my leg." The father said he'd gladly cut off an arm. The daughter said she'd remove her ear. The son said he'd cut off all his hair, and perhaps a foot, too. They let the baby be.

"We need a head," said the town executioner.

"Fine," said the father. "I will also deliver my nose."

This seemed to satisfy the executioner, so after all the other people were killed, the family was cut up and the pieces were laid out on the ground in their correct places to make a partial person who was the sacrifice to the kingdom's population control. The town dispersed, disoriented, unsure how to mourn their losses.

The cut-up family, after recovering, still made their sausage rolls, but no one could stand to buy them anymore because it was so disturbing to go into the store and see the noseless father, with that strap around his face, or watch the legless mother hop in to ring up the cash register, or to have to shout the order at the daughter since she only had one ear left. The family, broke, was forced to leave. They moved to the next town, which wasn't so bad after all, and opened up a new business, and since no one there had ever seen them whole, here they accepted the family of pieces without a problem and bought sausage rolls day after day. Each family member lived a long long time, and only the baby, who was complete, contracted any disease. When she did, at age twenty, they nursed her and nursed her until her leg fell off with gangrene, and then they had a party to celebrate her arrival.

That's the story my father told me at bedtime on my tenth birthday.

part one

20

On my twentieth birthday, I bought myself an ax.

This was the best gift I got in a decade. Before I saw it, shining on the wall of the hardware store like a lover made from steel and wood, I'd given up completely on the birthday celebration.

On my nineteenth, my mother had kicked me out of the house.

On my eighteenth, I had a party of two people, and after an hour, both claimed allergies, and went home, sneezing.

On my seventeenth, I made myself a chocolate cake, but since I didn't really want to eat it, stirred bug poison in with the mix. It rose beautifully, the best ever, and when I took it out of the oven, a perfect brown dome, I just circled the pan for a few hours, breathing in that warm buttery air. Some ants ate the crumbs on the counter and died.

On my sixteenth, my aunt sent me a beautiful scarlet silk dress, which smelled and felt as delicate as the inside of a wrist. Stroking it in my lap, I sifted through the phone book, finally picking out the name of a woman who lived at an address with 16s in it. Then I mailed the dress to her. Red is not my color.

On my fifteenth, fourteenth, thirteenth, twelfth, and eleventh birthdays, my mother and I went shopping, and each year, by the end, one of us was in tears of frustration because I didn't like anything, and I said I really didn't want anything, except, maybe, a new math workbook. You had to send away for those. They came from a big number barn in the South. My mother shook her head; she refused, flat-out, to buy me math supplies for my birthday, so finally we just put the money in the bank instead.

The year of my tenth birthday was when my father got sick, and that's when I started to quit.

I'd always loved the sound of pianos, so I signed up for lessons and took them for six weeks, and at the end of six weeks we had a recital. I wore a dress and played a minuet and my two hands were doing two different things at the same time and when it was over I drank juice and got hugged and the melody crooned inside my head. I walked my piano teacher to her car, and she smiled at me, proud. The sky clamped down. I lowered my voice: Listen, I said, urgent. You are never, *ever* to set foot near this house again.

Her eyebrows pulled in, puzzled. Mona? she asked. What?

Thanks, I said. But this is the end of the line.

I told my mother it was too bad, wasn't it, that the one piano teacher was leaving our small town of no opportunity to become a rock star in the big city. Her eyes widened and she picked up the phone and my heart started pounding, but to my huge relief the piano teacher's machine picked up and my mother's message was vague, something like: Good luck and wow! and we wish you all the best.

Three weeks later, they ran into each other at the market. What they talked about, I have no idea.

I took dance class ten times, and on the afternoon of my first leap, donated my ballet shoes to charity. I had one boyfriend and within two months had hardened into a statue in bed. I ran track like a shooting star and shot myself straight out of orbit.

I quit dessert to see if I could do it—of course I could; I quit breathing one evening until my lungs overruled; I quit touching my skin, sleeping with both hands under the pillow. When no one was home, I tied ropes around the piano, so that it would take me thirty minutes with scissors to get back to that minuet. Then I hid all the scissors.

I did not stop knocking on wood, which I did all the time, as a way to seal each quit into roots and bark; listen: I tell the wood—look at what I'm doing here. Mark this down. Notice.

No piano. No dessert. No track. Nothing. I am in love with stopping.

It's a fine art, when you think about it. To quit well requires an intuitive sense of beauty; you have to feel the moment of turn, right when desire makes an appearance, here is the instant to be severed, whack, this is the moment where quitting is ripe as a peach turning sweet on the vine: snap, the cord is cracked, peach falls to the floor, black and silver with flies.

I had one boyfriend. He was distracted most of the time but we stood in his front doorway on a warm summer night and his lips moved over my skin like a string quartet and I could feel that peach ready to shake off the tree.

I quit going to the movies.

I quit my job at the local diner when the chef kept going on and on about what a good runner I'd been.

I quit egg salad.

I quit flipping through atlases.

I'd long quit the idea of living away from home when, on that nineteenth birthday, my mother threw me out of the house. She closed the town tourist office that she owned and ran, came home early, and said: Mona, happy birthday, my present to you is this. Putting her hands on my shoulders, she marched me out the front door, and stood me on the lawn.

I love you, she said, but you are too old to live here.

But I love it here, I said.

Her hair blew around in the air. You're lying, she said, and what's worse is that you don't even know it.

I wasn't sure if she was adamant or just a lot of talk until she rolled my bed into the front hallway. My father, confused, just sidled around the sloppy pillow and comforter, and for two nights, I dreamt in the space where wall nearly met wall. On the second morning, I woke, went to the bathroom, came back, and found the bed was gone again. And the front door was open. My mother stood in the doorway, her back to me, shoulders lifting and lowering from laughter at the sight of it, covers rumpled, standing in the middle of the front lawn like a cow.

So I'll sleep out there then, I said, heading toward it.

She caught me in her arms and held me close. I could feel the laughter, warm in her arms and her chest.

I went apartment hunting that Saturday. My mother was off at work, but before I left, my father called to me from the living room. He was feeling feverish, and lay on the couch, a washcloth sprawled on his forehead like the limp flag of a defeated country. Central heating, he advised. Do you need anything? I asked, but he shook his head. And Mona, he said, make sure you get a place with a toilet that flushes. I nodded. I brought him a glass of water before I left.

The whole idea of moving made me nervous, so I kept company with the number 19 as I walked around town by myself. 19: the third centered hexagonal number. A prime. The amount of time alive of my chin, my toes, my brain. I wandered through the tree-lined streets, to the edge of town where the gray ribbon of highway dressed the hills in the distance like a lumpy yellow gift. I did pass a few FOR RENT signs, but the apartment I finally chose was only three blocks from my parents' house, sparkled with color, came with a toilet so powerful it could flush socks, and had an address that I liked: 9119.

The day I moved in, I placed my furniture pretty much where it had been at home. My bed, formerly grayish from the dimmed atmosphere of my parents' house, was already picking up its old pink tones. I hadn't seen it pink for nine years, and it looked like the color ads in newspapers that retain a steely quality of black-and-white even though they're newly splotched with reds and blues.

I called my mother when the phone was hooked up.

I'm here, I said. What now?

She was eating something crunchy. Decorate, she told me. Have a party.

The blank walls loomed white and empty. I ran through the rooms and said my name in each one.

Mona, I told the kitchen.

Mona, I whispered into the hall closet.

When it hit eleven o'clock, I put myself into the bed I'd slept in my entire life, in a room I'd never slept in, ever, and switched off the lights. The shadows made moving dark spirits on the walls, and I reached over to the potted tree my mother had given me as a housewarming present, and knocked on the trunk. I knocked and knocked. I didn't knock just a few times, I knocked maybe fifty.

One hundred knocks. More knocks. One hundred and fifty. More. I stopped and then something felt wrong, my stomach felt wrong, so I knocked some more.

The new place held its own around me, learning. This is me, I wanted to tell it. Hello. This is me protecting the world.

I knocked until midnight. I'd finish and then go back for more. This is how I imagine drugs are. You close in on the wood, pull in your breath, and you want to get it just right and your whole body is taut, breath held, tight with getting it just right and awaiting the release—*ssss*—which lasts about five seconds and when it's over it's not right again yet, more, you need to go back. Just one more time. Just one more time and I'll get it exactly right this time and be done for the rest of my life.

O̲nce I was all settled in, and each drawer had a purpose, and the bathroom was well-stocked with toilet paper and window cleaner, I invited my mother over for lunch.

My father sent his apologies, but didn't come with her; he was feeling off again; this happened. I served turkey sandwiches using the same brands of mayonnaise, mustard, and bread that my mother bought. After we ate, she brought a bag of cherries from her purse, and asked if I wanted to initiate the apartment by spitting cherry pits out the window. I said no thanks. Years ago, we used to go into their backyard in summertime and perch on the grass and spit cherry pits as far as we could. My mother's spits were badly aimed and ricocheted off to the left; my father was the better spitter, but my learning curve was sharp and I watched him close as those reddish ovals went flying. After he got sick, I did some spitting by myself, which was not very fun, and spit with my mother, which was not very challenging, and once I got him to join me and for some reason he breathed in too quick and the pit went backward and got lodged in his throat. Cherry pits are small, and so it was just three or four seconds of that thick labyrinth breathing but enough to scare us both into shaking. I stopped popping whole cherries in my mouth and took to biting down to pit and eating around that. My father cut his food into tiny pieces.

Before she left 9119, my mother put those cherries, bright as blood cells, on the counter, took out a camera, and snapped some photos of the rooms to show my father later.

I had sex with that one boyfriend. Once. Twice. All at his place. His skin was a buoyant ship over mine, and he kissed silver into the back of my neck, and was fine with my insistence on having lights ON at all times. I like to see what's happening, I explained. Cool, he said, picking at his elbow. After the third time, when we were just starting to get the hang of it, I came home one morning to my new empty apartment; I checked my messages to see if anyone had died while I was out in the world having sex but no one had or at least it was unreported so I sat on the couch and kept a knock going on the side table when I thought of how his eyelashes made a simple black rim when he looked down.

The clock said noon so I went into the kitchen and opened the refrigerator but the food inside looked too complicated and I peered into the cupboards but I didn't want turkey soup, or garbanzo beans, or tuna, and I wandered into the bathroom and without even really thinking about it unwrapped the spare package of soap that I kept in the cabinet beneath the sink.

I bought the same brand my mother did. A bright white bar, rocking on its back, friendly. I brought it to the living room couch, and held it for a while, smelling it, and there was a knife sitting on the side table from the previous day's apple, which seemed convenient, and after a few minutes of just holding and smelling, I picked up the knife, balanced the bar on the arm of the couch, sawed off a portion, set it sailing in my mouth, and bit down.

Slide! Slip! It careened around my tongue. Gave like chocolate under my teeth. I cut another piece. My mouth crammed with froth. Mmm. I cut again. My hand slipped. I steadied the knife, cut again.

I'd chewed half the bar before I realized that it tasted strange, that the feeling it left in my mouth was not right, that there was something about the swallowing part that was wrong. By then it was making me gag and I went to the bathroom where the mirror revealed lather gathered around lip corners in clusters. Sticking the remains of the bar in the shower, I gulped glass after glass of water, spitting up foam into the sink, and the rest of the day I thought very little of the boyfriend, and instead wandered the rooms, burping clean burps, evaluating how badly I felt: Should I just relax? Should I get my stomach pumped?

When I woke up the next morning, slightly dizzy but not dead, I stumbled into the shower and stood in the spray: meek, naked, distant. I used the straight bitten end of the soap to clean myself, but before I put it back on its shelf, I took one mildly interested nibble. The smell slammed back through me. In an instant, my stomach heaved up and I crouched down, water sticking in my eyes, and threw up down the drain, all whiteness and foam, soap rushing in waves back through me.

Then I took that remaining bar, complete with the paneled markings of my teeth, and dumped it into the trash.

I couldn't use soap for months after that—had to wash my hands with shampoo. A week or so later, when I next saw the

boyfriend, he took his hand up my shirt and clicked my bra, releasing my breasts, but I stepped away and told him no. Peach fell
off the tree, dead. He blinked; oh, he said, okay. If I had any
doubts, if I felt the warmth rising when he touched the corner of
my lips with the tip of his finger, when he kissed the nape of my
neck, turning my entire back into perforation, I just excused myself, went into the bathroom and washed my hands. He used the
same brand of soap I did, and the smell did the trick right away. I
left his house before midnight, underpants wet, stomach roiling,
knocking every sidewalk tree. We broke up about three weeks later.
He kept saying he was sorry. I held my clean fingers to my
nose, nodded.

After all that, the one thing I loved but never quit, could not seem
to give up, was, of all things, math. I tried to stop thinking about
numbers but found myself, against my will, adding my steps and
multiplying the people in the park against one another, knocking
on wood in a careful rhythm, counting endlessly: sheep, students,
parents, age, heartbeats. Mix up some numbers and signs, and you
get an equation for the way the wind shifts or an axiom for the
movement of water, or the height of someone, or for how skin
feels. You can account for softness. You can explain everything.
Even air is just an arrangement of digits, and with just the right
balance—poof! We breathe.

You can find all the letters of atheist in the word mathematics,
but if you ask me, it's just the opposite.

I've spent entire afternoons thinking about one number, flying
down its long onyx tunnel, opening up the trapdoor that it is. Take
5. Seems regular—five-dollar bill, five-minute break—but five is

also the sum of two squares, and a prime, and pentagrams, and my sixth-grade math teacher told me that the Pythagoreans thought 5 was about marriage because it was 3 (their first odd) joined with 2 (their first even). For my parents' anniversary that year, I made them five small cakes. They seemed puzzled (maybe because it was their twenty-first anniversary) but my mother praised the frosting, in chocolate peaks on her fingertips.

I noticed the 31 flag they gave me at the sandwich shop, so then I knew how many sandwiches I had to wait for before I ate my own. I used the 60–90 dial on the heat thermometer to calm my goose bumps or cool my sweat. I poked the little squares 1–9 on the telephone keypad to dial up the world; I knocked 15 times on the potted tree before I fell asleep. 2-hour parking signs told me how to avoid tickets, and I memorized the capacity warning in the elevator: only 22 allowed. Beautiful. Clear. To quit numbers would be to pack in a bustling group of 25 people, eager to get where they're going, let the metal doors shut, and plunge straight into the basement cement, swift and hard as a comet.

2

I heard about a woman who got a job reordering an entire town. The numbers were off because the mayor had a counting problem, and she'd been hired to come in and reintroduce 8. It'd been missing in some clocks. She'd also needed to go over the books and see if the adding was correct (which of course it wasn't, without 8) and to check all the signs. Drivers were apparently getting off the highway, following the sign that said GAS: 2 MILES, to find nothing but dusty roads. The sign was supposed to say 88. It was a whole industry, townsfolk dashing over to gasless cars with cans of portable petrol.

She was called a number doctor. That was my dream job.

But I was still intrigued and humbled when I got a call from the elementary school principal asking me if I wanted to be the new math teacher. At the last minute, the previous math teacher had flown off to Paraguay. No one knew where she was until her resignation arrived, four days before school began, in the form of a postcard with very green trees on the front. Sorry, she'd written, but I have decided to become a revolutionary. Please send my final paycheck to this address.

It's *dreadful*, the principal said to me on the phone. You have no idea how hard it is to find a math teacher.

She said she was sleepless with worry until she remembered, in a dreamlike flash, a summer years and years before when she was in the park and happened upon me, curled up by the duck pond, sipping lemonade, doing long division.

You're it, she said.

I've never taught math before, I said. I'm only nineteen.

So, she said. Know how to add?

I laughed.

Or an octagon, she said, how about octagons?

What about them?

What are they? she asked.

I leaned against the counter. I'm not an idiot, I said. I'm practically married to the stop sign, I said.

And can you start Monday? she asked. Because you're hired, Mona Gray.

She hung up before I could answer.

The elementary school was a quick brisk walk from my apartment. I went to look at it that weekend, passing the red mouth of the fire station, striding by the house with the dumb iron geese on the lawn, trudging through an overgrown empty lot. Above the rooftops, leaving a diamond of bluish shadow on the cement, loomed the large blue-glass hospital, the town's most unusual building. But that marked the other end of town. On one end: kid school. Other end: people coughing and dying and weak.

The school was a modest white box on a corner. Inside was a kitchen for the staff, a lobby area for lunch boxes and jackets, a big activity room, and a hall lined with doors. Each had a subject card on it: READING in red, SCIENCE in yellow, and mine said MATH in big black letters. I spent a minute with the word, proud, and then took a breath and went inside.

I was very disappointed to see that the math classroom had no windows and was the width of a hallway. Also it smelled like concrete. ART and SPELLING were squarer, and windowed, and scented with sunshine, so I figured math gets the shaft in classroom selection because the math teacher is the dentist of the school curriculum. It's a miracle if there are kids in the class who don't hate you.

Except me. I had loved all my math teachers. I'd loved my arithmetic teacher with the giraffe face who made up word problems that rhymed; I'd loved the woman who wept when she explained quadratic equations because, she said, their beauty was so true it was what fashion magazines should do their photo shoots on; I'd loved the eager substitute with the paint-splattered ties who held a contest for finding a perfect circle in nature that I won by pointing to my pupil.

I'd loved my high school algebra teacher the most—the man who now ran the local hardware store instead. Mr. Jones had been a huge presence to me, growing up, a young girl, attracted to numbers. He lived next door to my parents, and I'd never seen him without a wax number hanging from a string around his neck. They varied, according to his mood—he'd go higher if in a better mood, lower if he felt lower. Generally he hung steady around 15. Only once did I see it go up to 37, and that same day a woman exited his door in the early morning, and they kissed long in the doorway and he seemed like a stranger, a dashing shadow of himself. Only a few times did it go so low as 2. On those days he just went outside to take out the trash, and that's all I saw of him. He was in the house, probably wearing that 2, for several weeks. His classes had math substitutes the entire time, and all testing was postponed until Jones felt better.

He'd been the best and worst of them all.

So that weekend, to honor all math teachers, I transformed my ugly classroom into a beautiful museum of numbers, but on the first day of school, the kindergarten and first grade ignored everything. They were cute enough in their overalls and hair bows, and a couple of them called me mom by accident, but they didn't even glance at the walls and notice the carefully framed construction-paper numbers I'd slaved over all weekend: Demure blue 2! Fun red 5! Noble black 10! The Rules of the Universe laid out in front of them! Just, as of yet, unorganized. Two peed and one thought he had a hurt finger and I thought it looked just like a regular finger but he wanted very badly to go to the nurse who turned out to be his aunt so I let him.

My own enthusiasm was sinking when the bell rang for third period and no one came in.

This wasn't a bad thing. I thought it was nice to have a break. I checked the schedule but it said no, I had the second grade now. I read the roster, in my boss's well-slanted cursive:

SECOND GRADE:

John Beeze

Ann DiLanno

Elmer Gravlaki

Mimi Lunelle

Danny O'Mazzi

Lisa Venus

Ellen (last name?)

The last was written in an embarrassed scrawl. I practiced the names. The second bell rang. I erased the board.

After five minutes, I opened the door and peered into the hall. Bingo. Right outside the classroom was a clump of seven seven-year-olds, laying on the floor.

Are you the second grade? I asked. Come on, I said. I have you for math now!

A ratty-haired girl poked her head off the ground and looked at me. The rest rolled back and forth. Only three were wearing the requisite first-day name tags.

I cleared my throat and was about to start the year with a bang by sending a couple of them straight to the boss when they jumped up and went straight in to my wall of numbers.

The girl with ratty hair pointed to big purple 3.

I'm Lisa Venus, she said. This one's the best.

Her friend, name tag stating John Beeze, touched the foot of red 5. We smiled at each other.

Good morning! I said. I'm Ms. Gray, your new math teacher. Let me tell you, I said, math can be a wonderful subject—

One boy with a name tag, Elmer Gravlaki, dove under the table. Another with no name tag and a cap of black hair made his hands into guns and shot everybody.

Lisa Venus walked the row of portraits, a tiny docent.

Don't like 2, she said. I like the yellow 9 a lot. I don't like 7. I like the 4. Don't like the 1.

Sit, I said.

Gun boy found the drawers I'd filled with counting devices—buttons and paper clips and rubber bands.

Our last math teacher had a nervous breakdown, said Mimi Lunelle, sitting at her desk with curls that made perfect whirlpools, like she was constantly spinning down a drain.

No, I said. She went to Paraguay to become a revolutionary. I'm Ms. Gray.

Paraguay? Mimi asked.

You already said your name, muttered the sour-faced girl next to Mimi.

Paraguay's a place, I said. Now, let's start with a game! First, tell me your name and favorite number!

No response.

Gun boy stuck a button in the crotch of a rubber band and pulled it taut.

Lisa Venus raised her hand.

Sit please, I said. She leaned on a chair.

I'm Lisa Venus, she said again. My favorite is a billion.

One to ten, I said. Hi Lisa.

Three, she said. Nine. Seven.

Come be three, I said. Do I have a second volunteer?

Gun boy aimed his rubber band right at me. Elmer whimpered under the table. The sour-faced girl twisted her lips with her fingers.

I hated teaching, suddenly.

My favorite is five, said John Beeze from his desk.

I had John and Lisa come up to the front and told them to physically form the numbers—Lisa sticking out her butt to get the second arch of the 3, John kicking up a heel to finish 5.

There! I said. So what's the total of Lisa and John?

The group groaned.

8, announced Lisa, head down.

Anyone want to be 8? I said.

To my surprise, gun boy raised his hand at the back of the room. He snapped the rubber band at the wall and the button tumbled down.

My favorite is 8, he said evenly.

And what's your name?

Danny O'Mazzi, he said.

His T-shirt sleeves stopped high on his shoulders and there were biceps showing in his arms, already, at age seven. After putting away the button and rubber band with unexpected neatness, he walked to the front of the room, and without any cueing from me, turned out his feet, bent his knees, and clasped his hands over his head.

Hey! I said, grinning. Great! Now who wants to be the plus sign?

Hands went up, waving. I brought Mimi Lunelle to the front and she held her feet together and spread her arms wide. This is good, I said. Now I loved teaching. I wished my boss would walk in. We had our first human equation and my spirits were rising and it would've worked beautifully if sour-face, the one named Ann DiLanno, hadn't started stomping her foot and muttering because she wanted to be the plus sign. I explained that Mimi Lunette (Lun-elle, spoke the plus sign) was already the plus sign but Ann DiLanno wouldn't settle down even when I offered her the very desirable role of equals sign. She kicked the table leg and Elmer started to cry and Danny O'Mazzi was making his arm into a rifle when, at Lisa's suggestion, we sat down.

I have an idea, Lisa said.

Shoot, I said.

Shoot! said Danny.

Lisa asked something like: What if we, how about if we, could we go make numbers in nature? When I asked her to explain what she meant, she stuttered and rambled. I know! said John Beeze, we can find numbers. I didn't know what that meant either but I was inspired by their eagerness, and wanted to keep them quiet, so on the spot, I made up Numbers and Materials.

Listen, I said. How's this.

The plan was for Fridays, and the idea was that one student would present a number, made out of a material, to the class, and subtract with it. After all, I said, this is the year you learn subtraction. Their faces grew grave. Subtraction is far more daunting than adding, due to all that borrowing business.

Who wants to begin? I asked.

Lisa's hand shot up and I told her to bring something good for Friday and we'd end the class with it and what a terrific way to start our weekend.

To my utter shock, the class quieted. We spent the rest of the class going over the addition they'd learned last year from Paraguay. They seemed sharp enough.

When the bell rang, they ran to recess and I slumped in a seat, kicking out my legs, already exhausted, but also laughing to myself, thinking of the look on Danny O'Mazzi's face when he bent his knees and wove his fingers together to take the shape of that 8. I liked them. I stayed there for fifteen minutes, peaceful and quiet, listening to the rubber roar of recess outside.

3

When I bought the ax at the hardware store, I had a fine time walking it through town, swinging the wooden handle, wondering where to keep it. I strolled those shaded sidewalks, trying it out in different rooms in my mind. Should I store it under the bed? Dangle it from the towel rack? Jam it in the silverware drawer? I would come home from work and visit my ax, open the closet and say hello, beautiful tool, the same way I do when I buy a new pair of shoes and want to greet them, standing in the closet, waiting patiently for their right occasion.

But when I did finally get home that night, at that point things had changed, and I was a trembling ball of worry, and didn't care much about storage anymore, and just shoved the ax under the kitchen sink next to the dishwashing detergent.

Regardless. Every young lady should have a weapon around the house.

On Friday of that first week, I was on a teaching break in the school kitchen, knocking up the wood wall, when a young man walked in with chemical-burn stains all over his arms. He had a steady back, standing at the sink, washing.

You're Ms. Gray, right? he said, over his shoulder.

I nodded, mute with concentration: knock knock knock knock, inhale, exhale, repeat.

He finished washing, arms speckled as a painting, then came over and reached out a damp hand to shake hello.

I'm Benjamin Smith, he said. I teach science.

He indicated the marks on his arms, as proof.

Math, I said, between knocks; Mona, I said.

He smiled at me. He smelled like soap.

About an hour later, halfway through my pumpkin-seed lesson with the second grade, Lisa Venus excused herself to the bathroom. I had just given each second-grader a pile of ten pumpkin seeds that I'd roasted the night before, and told them to take one away at a time and count what remained. Mimi of the whirlpool curls made her seeds into a heart shape. I heard crunching sounds under the table and squatted down. Elmer Gravlaki was settled on the carpet, busily chewing.

Hey, I said. Stop eating the math.

I'd barely noticed that Lisa had left, so busy was I telling Danny O'Mazzi to STOP flicking seeds at the wall, when she returned to class wearing a thin tube, one end connected to the other so that it made a loop, a clear crown resting high on her ratty head.

What's that? I asked when she walked back through the door. The class swiveled in their seats. They'd had enough of seeds.

An I.V., said Lisa. Get it? Those are my initials. Almost.

I looked closer. This was indeed the tube portion of an I.V.

Isn't it supposed to be saving someone? I asked.

She scoffed, softly. It's been used already, she said, walking to the front of the room.

Excuse me, she said, I am Princess Cancer.

I looked at her by the chalkboard wondering what she was doing. I didn't really like seeing that I.V. here in my math room, ripped out from someone's vein. Benjamin Smith the science teacher walked by, and who knew if he might peek in and call the hospital, report Lisa for stolen property. I went over and shut the door, knocking it gently.

Lisa gave a careful nod at the front, keeping the tube balanced.

I'm ready for Numbers and Materials, she said.

I blinked. Numbers and Materials?

Remember? she asked. We bring in numbers from the world of nature?

John piped in. Or things that just look like numbers.

I nodded. Of course! I said, half-remembering.

Lisa raised her hands and pointed to the see-through I.V. tiara on her head.

This is my zero, she said. From nature.

I remembered the assignment then, like a punch.

That's not nature, called sour-faced Ann DiLanno from her seat. That's plastic.

Lisa glared at Ann. Ann scowled at Lisa. Their mutual hatred had been developing all week like a man-eating fast-growing jungle fern.

Plastic comes from nature, Lisa said in the same royal tone.

It's man-made, said John Beeze.

And man is natural, said Lisa.

Ann rolled her eyes. Lisa resumed her pose of dignity. I walked to the back of the room to listen.

This is my zero from nature, she said. Zero times anything is zero, she told the class. Zero wins every fight. Zero demolishes the world.

The world is shaped like zero, said Danny O'Mazzi.

Exactly, said Lisa, smiling. Danny made *pow-wow* sounds in his chair.

Subtract, please, I said.

She nodded. The I.V. caught the overhead light and glinted.

$20 - 0 = 20$, she said. $4 - 0 = 4$. Ten billion trillion $- 0 =$ ten billion trillion.

Good, I said, still thinking of that I.V. bag, right beside a dehydrated unmedicated person but unable to connect. Saline dripping to the floor. The hospital summons the janitor. Where is it? they ask. He shrugs. I have no use for an I.V. tube, he says, but his hands twist when he's nervous and the dehydrated man is thirsty and mad.

$250 \times 0 = 0$! Lisa said.

No multiplication yet, I said, knocking on the wood bookcase. You're getting ahead of yourself.

She grumbled, but did a few more, subtracting. When she was done she asked for questions.

What does I.V. mean? asked one.

Intra-venous, said Lisa.

Lisa Venus, said John. Lisa smiled.

So we'll call you Intra, said Ann DiLanno.

That's fine, said Lisa. I think that's pretty, she said.

Ann raised her hand. I have a question for Intra. Intra?

Who goes next time? someone asked.

Ann kept talking. I intra-duce Intra, she said. This is Intra. Everyone say hello to Intra.

The class mumbled a hello and I said, That was good Lisa, thanks! That was our very first Numbers and Materials, who wants to go next week?

Elmer Gravlaki raised his hand underneath the table, which made a thunking sound, and I said he could go only if he'd sit in a chair from now on. He said, muffled, that he already knew exactly what he would bring. John raised his hand too so I told him to bring something to show at recess as a supplement.

Does it have to be in order? asked Ellen, the one so quiet I always forgot her. The one without a last name.

I guess not, I said.

I turned to the front. Lisa stood, waiting.

Sit down Intra, said Ann.

I told Ann we'd had enough from her.

Lisa kept standing there, nostrils flaring slightly. We didn't have enough time for anything else, so as we cleaned up the seeds I let her show how zero, when doubled, could make quite an unusual bracelet.

The bell rang and the class ran out, Ann yelling: Bye Intra! in her flattest, meanest voice, and while Lisa was packing her bag I called her to the back of the room. She half-skipped up to me, crowned, the lightest I'd seen her yet. I asked her where she'd gotten an I.V. in the first place, and that's when she told me about her mother. She's got really bad cancer and wears a red wig, she said, doing little kicks with her feet. Lisa's hair was so ratty it barely moved when she did.

She'll die in less than a year, Lisa said. Is that it?

A year? I said. She nodded vigorously.

She's got no hair left, she said.

Are you doing okay? I asked.

Lisa started puffing her cheeks, in and out.

What kind of cancer? I asked.

She smiled a little. Guess, she said.

Lung? She shook her head. Skin? I said. No. Brain? No. Bone? No. Mouth? No. Breast? No. Colon? No. Throat? No. Blood? No. Liver? No. Pancreas? No.

What's left? I asked.

She leaned in, conspiratorially. Eye cancer, she said, winking.

I've never heard of that, I said.

Lisa nodded. It's brand-new, she said. My mom is one of the first. They're doing lots of tests. It spreads really fast.

Is there anything I can do? I asked.

She let all the breath out of her cheeks, leaned in, and looked at the skin around my eyes. Your eyes are like little blue zeroes, she said. $2 - 0 = 2$, she said.

My eyes aren't blue, I said. They're more gray than blue.

They're more blue, she said.

I put my knuckles on the chair seat.

I like the name Intra, she said. I hate Ann DiLanno. Are you sick? she asked. Her face was bright.

It took me a second to catch up with her sentences, and then I did another knock on the wooden chair seat. What do you mean? I said. I'm fine, I said.

She told me my class was already her favorite class and that if I really wanted to do something for her, then I should not get sick, ever.

But sometimes I get a cold, I said. People get colds.

She adjusted the I.V. and glued her eyes on me.

I *never* get colds, she said.

And even though the plastic on her head was fogged and dirty, and her hair was a nest, and she was not yet four feet tall, she was hard with poise right then, and I felt myself shrink in my chair. Oh, I said. Well. Intra is a perfectly good name, I mumbled.

I didn't know what else to say and now I wanted her to leave so I thanked her again for being such a good starting act for Numbers and Materials and told her to go to recess. She said she loved Numbers and Materials more than anything in any class, even more than Hands-on Health in Science, and ran out of the room.

I blew my nose and knocked some more and kept knocking and thought: she wears the news on her head.

Welcome back to school. My summer vacation was bad.

4

I had been ten years old and quitting nothing at the time when my skin-doctor father walked into the living room one day in August with death perched on his shoulder as high and pleased as an organ grinder's monkey.

His voice was quiet. Help, he said.

The rest of us—three—were on the living-room couch. I was sitting with my rich aunt, my mother's sister, looking at a sportswear and lingerie catalog she'd brought for her visit. My mother was cleaning out her purse. At the sound of his overwound voice, we all looked up.

Arthur, said my mother, fingers laced with gum wrappers, what's wrong?

His face was gray. Truly, actually gray. All six eyes, the female majority in the house, fixed onto his, which were tight with fear and glittering silver.

That first time, even my clearheaded aunt got worried. She was the head of a hotshot metal corporation in the big city, and very directive. She said: Go to the emergency room. She said: *Do* it. The force in her voice pushed tears to my eyes.

My mother, lips together, led my father to the car. Just the day before, he and I had gone to the big green high school track, sang to the radio together in the car, and raced each other. I watched the way his feet hit the ground—heel, earth, toe—and he was so quick but I was faster than I'd ever been before and one time, I almost, *almost* won. He laughed when he saw me chasing his heels, and afterward we had orange drinks at the diner and he told the waiter my name was Miss Speedy.

I pulled up a chair to the kitchen table and joined my aunt, who sat there with her catalog. We tried to focus on the clothes. She pointed out a skirt—long and straight and dark red—and I nodded but have since felt a wave of terror in stores when I've seen any relative of that skirt hanging on the racks. My tears were big and splatted directly on the models, fat drops that made their paper stomachs buckle.

My parents were gone for four hours. One hour. Two hours. Three hours. Four hours.

My aunt, overworked, fell asleep on the catalog.

Four hours and ten minutes.

Four hours and eleven minutes.

Four hours and twelve minutes.

I held my knees and watched the clock over the stove shuffle and restructure its red digital lines.

Both my parents returned from the hospital at the tail end of the fifth hour, and my father still looked gray and now my mother, too, looked grayer. My aunt was still asleep on her catalog, but I was wide awake and I went over and hugged my mother because I was too afraid to hug him. He looked like he might be leaking. That ashy stuff, smoking out into the air. But he was upright, he was walking, and he was alive.

Your father's okay, my mother said. He didn't look over at me and left the room. I heard the mattress in their bedroom sigh and sink as he lay down.

It wasn't a stroke? muttered my aunt, shaking awake.

It wasn't anything, said my mother. The doctor did a lot of tests and he's fine.

What do you mean? I asked.

She shook her head.

What was it? my aunt asked, standing.

My mother opened the refrigerator, and stuck a spoon in a jar of peanut butter.

So, she said. What did you two do while we were gone?

My aunt marched out of the kitchen, and I heard her low voice speaking to my father who, as far as I could tell, wasn't responding. I lifted the catalog from the table and ran a hand over it, bumpy from my tears. A record of four very bad hours. I held it up to my mother, to show her, to shove it in her face, but her eyes were focused somewhere else. She took a second spoon from the drawer and made me a peanut-butter lollipop too.

Is he dying? I asked, in the smallest voice possible.

She put down her spoon. No, honey, she said, touching my hair. I don't think so.

I nodded. I smiled. That's good, I said.

She poured two glasses of milk into two wineglasses. We drank. Her eyes, over the top of the wineglass, rain-colored against milk foam, looked sad and tired.

What is it? I said to her, putting down my glass. Are you keeping something from me? Tell me the truth, I said. I am ten years old.

But my mother just shook her head again.

They complimented his cholesterol levels, she said. His blood pressure is low.

What's wrong with him? I asked, leaning forward, gripping the glass stem.

Nothing, she said.

By the next evening, my father was still alive and walking and he seemed to be in a slightly better mood, but I didn't see him regain brightness and color, ever. We never went back to the track. He stopped singing with the radio. I walked so much faster than him now that the name Miss Speedy felt disgusting in its rightness. My aunt stayed a few more days, even going to the doctor's office to drum up more information, but she returned with nothing but a dinner date. She took me shopping that week on the street of stores and bought me a turquoise jacket that she said was so cute and matched my eyes but halfway home I said it was the ugliest thing I'd ever seen. The rest of the walk was silent and deadly. She decided to cut her stay short. Judy, she asked my mother, do you really need me here? My mother shook her head, using a toothpick to spear kernels from a tin can of corn. A few days after my aunt had driven away, when I was sure she'd be home, I ripped out three pages from the warped lingerie catalog and mailed them to her; I circled several of the bras that were clearly the wrong size and wrote, in black pen: I bet these would look great on you. She wrote back after a month and said everyone in the big city was wearing the jacket I'd returned. I swiped my father's tissue after he'd sneezed and mailed her that.

At home, brightness seemed to be draining from the house. The orange carpet paled to beige. The burgundy sofa looked more nut-colored to me now. Brass quintets on the stereo sounded like drawers of silverware, clanking. No one read the glossy magazines on the coffee table anymore: What was the point of an alarm clock shaped like a turtle? I saved a page for posterity, but dumped the rest of the lingerie catalog.

The warmth of afternoon, squares of sunlight, glowing reds— all of this darkened; it was as if someone had installed a dim switch on the side of our house and spun it down to Low.

I didn't know what to do about it, so I just got used to it. When I saw myself in a mirror at school, my eyes were blue and my tongue was red. I looked garish and over-made-up to myself, with blue eyes. Blue eyes! I knocked on trees as I walked home, thinking of the gall of my body, having eyes the color of the stupid sky. At home, the mirror in the bathroom reflected back a more acceptable shade of industrial lead. When I saw pairs of ducks in the pond at the park, each time I convinced myself that the female, brown and beige, was more beautiful than the male. She was direct, and simple. I ignored that male duck, whose iridescent green feathers I now found ostentatious.

I did not remind myself that only two years before I had written a ballad about mallards on my walk to school, about how those feathers held the empress's hidden emeralds, so she could always get money if she needed it.

My father managed to go to work every day, to the blue glass hospital where he cured people of skin disease. To his office he wore dark blazers over dull shirts over tweed pants. His watchband was silver; his wedding ring, white gold. His thick black hair now had stripes of age in it, and his eye whites were thin as skim milk. I had to go see him at work once because I needed an itch cream for my knuckles, which were so overknocked they'd broken out, and when I entered his office, he was standing by his secretary. She was a woman who believed strongly in the powers of herbal tea and singing. She wore a dress the color of cranberry juice and sported huge earrings shaped like birdcages that held inside them miniature plastic parrots. I was struck, held still at the door, by the contrast.

I waved to the secretary, who handed me a lollipop even though I was too old then; it was grape, a purple circle. I unwrapped it and popped it into my mouth. The secretary offered the bowl of lollipops to my father, as a joke. To both of our surprise, he reached in and fished around.

Aha! he said, when he pulled out his choice.

It would've made sense to laugh but it just wasn't funny. He'd selected the only black licorice lollipop left over from the last batch that'd had patients complaining. He ripped off the plastic and held it up in his hand. I could feel the secretary trying to get eye contact with me, birdcages swinging, but I wouldn't look over. I didn't want to know the expression on her face.

5

That hospital where my father worked was the one true attraction in town. Everything else was very regular—we had a town hall, a library, one high school, a park. A butcher, a baker, an auto shop, an ice-cream store. All the buildings were one story high, and one story out loud. At the tourist agency, smack in the center of the park, in the center of town, my mother kept her people informed by busily making brochures called *History of the Bug Shop* or *Evolution of Our Gas Station*. There was also a record of everyone who had ever left town and where they were now. Supposedly Molly Glee, who I'd gone to high school with, was currently in Sweden, making boats. I thought this was a big load of bull. My personal feeling was that there was a whole lot of lying that went on about where people were once they left. No one wanted to admit their kid had ridden off into that glorious western sunset only to sell insurance in another small town in the middle of another nowhere.

But even if it was true. Everything was eclipsed anyway, by the clear blue shadows of that hospital.

Its architecture would've been ornate anywhere, but especially

in such a small town. Some very wealthy, slowly dying architect
from the South had come many years before and built it entirely of
blue glass, hoping to heal himself with the dry climate, and also to
make life for the local sick people more beautiful. The hospital was
twelve stories high, the biggest building in town by far. The clear-
cut blue-glass elevator was so thick it made the world look like liquid, and since there was no body of water around for miles, this
was the closest you could get to swimming.

A month or so after he finished his masterpiece, the architect
died, in a transparent blue room he designed himself, top floor,
doing his best to replicate heaven.

My mother remembered the whole thing. She'd been just a
teenager when the architect had come to town. She often told me
about watching truck after truck drive in from the highway and
head straight to the empty dirt lot, truck beds loaded with walls of
blue glass—thick, clear panes of hardened sky. The hospital took
seven years to build. My mother said the process was wonderful,
from frame to completion, and as the walls and windows shot
higher and higher, blue shadows large as swimming pools on the
pavement, the whole town watched in awe from below.

On the day of the grand opening, in fact, Mr. George O'Mazzi,
a war veteran, future father of biceped Danny, slammed his arm
deliberately in a car door because he wanted the distinction of
being the first to sleep overnight in the new blue palace. The
brand-new ambulance spun down the street, jaunty and clean,
red light awhirl. Mr. O'Mazzi's plan failed miserably, however,
because although the exterior was in great shape, there was
very little equipment and even fewer doctors inside the hospital
at the time, so he spent hours in terrible pain before those

trucks pulled in from the highway again, this time piled high with drugs.

When asked the following week by my blue-eyed mother just exactly what it was like to sleep in there, for the brochure on *History of the Hospital*, he stared at her. Like spending the night inside your eyeball, he said. Except imagine a needle poking right through the pupil.

She blinked.

Unfortunately, his injured arm, already weak and damaged from shrapnel, got infected from the car-door slam, and had to be removed. After his recovery, Mr. O'Mazzi brought the separated arm to the town glassmaker, who sealed it inside a rectangle of the same blue glass, for proud display on their mantel, engraved with the words FIRST SURGERY.

Word of the hospital's beauty spread, and attracted doctors from all over the country. Some came to town, balked at the size of the population, and left; but others, like my father, were soothed by the climate and sense of space, and stayed. He was glad to get away from his side of the country, a place so cold in wintertime that bullies went after scarves instead of lunch money.

My mother and father met right away because he was new and wanted to get connected and she was the best-informed resident. He explained to her how he fixed hives and halted acne; she told him how the town had saved the old oak tree on Maiden Lane from blight. Their first kiss was by the duck pond when the very first ducklings had been dropped off, by some traveler from a city of excess birds.

They held their wedding in the park, ducklings now ducks, and invited whoever wanted to come. The wedding album looks like a town fair. My mother reminds me of a dove, her skirts lifting and rustling off the page, a bow-shaped smile on her face. The hospital looms in the background, shimmering blue as an upright pond on a bright sunlit summer afternoon.

That first year my father got sick, my parents told me over dinner that we weren't taking a vacation that year. We'd had a plan to go down a river in a boat.

Your father is uncomfortable leaving his doctors, my mother explained, twisting the end of her napkin into a spear.

But the doctors say nothing, I said.

My mother pointed her paper spear at me and jabbed at the air with it. True, she said.

Well I don't care, I said immediately. I looked over to my father for approval, but he wasn't looking at me; he was looking out the window at something else. After cleaning up, I went into my bed-room and took out my homework, and when I heard them walk into other rooms and settle down, I thought: well, the truth is, vacations are pointless anyway, because you always have to come back, so you might as well just save time, skip the middle step, and stay put in the first place.

My mother sat in the living room, alone. I heard her shift the books around, sighing a bit. She didn't know yet that from now on, we would be roping ourselves in by the borders of the town because my father worried he might die out in the open somewhere.

I would like to die on my own soil, he told my mother after the fifth year of making no plans to leave, even for an afternoon.

Oh, you're not going to die, she'd answered, flat. And besides, she said. This isn't even your own soil.

When my father spoke, his voice was gentle.

If you want, Judy, my father said, you can go by yourself. You can bring a camera and show me photos.

She'd seemed unmoved throughout the conversation but that's when I heard her voice crack in half.

But I want to go with you, she said.

It was the youngest I ever heard her sound.

That first night of not leaving, my mother called to me from her post in the living room. I was nestled in my bedroom, math textbook open in my lap, cross-legged on the bed. Mona, she called out, pick a page! What do you mean? I garbled, chewing on the side of a yellow pencil. Just pick, she said. I looked down at the page I was on: Dividing Fractions. I pulled the pencil from my teeth. Page 68, I called out. She made a paper flipping sound and then I heard her laugh. Kentucky, she announced, pick another. I made 68 into a fraction: $^6/_8$ and slimmed it down: $^3/_4$. 34, I called out. 34! Flip flip flip. Chile! she said. What are you doing? I asked, and she said: More pages, give me more! I checked my sheet of answers and picked out numbers. 33. 12? 27! Oh, she said, such good choices, she said. Would you rather see Paris or Hawaii? Paris! I yelled back. Paris! No wait, I said, Hawaii! Dark blue ocean and volcanoes. Hawaii! I hollered. Page 100, I suggested. There were more page-flipping sounds. Oooh, my mother said, oooh. What? I asked, emerging from my room. My mother was curled up on the formerly burgundy sofa and had, in her lap, the huge hardbacked brown atlas we'd bought for a buck at the Finch's garage sale. She held up the map to me, page 100. Corsica, she said. Now that must be incredible. Orange blossoms and sharp cliffs and lasagna too.

I tucked myself up on the sofa next to my mother. Show me, I said.

She outlined the borders of the island. The Tyrrhenian Sea, she said, doesn't that sound great? *Tyr-rhe-ni-an*. She released the word slowly, letting the back of her hand glide over my hair, knuckles combing my scalp. Let's go tomorrow, she said.

I pulled closer. Where's Japan? I asked.

We'll make it a world tour, my mother said. First, Tokyo. Then Nepal. Uruguay. How about Morocco? She flipped the pages fast and countries blurred by in calm pastels. She pointed out Casablanca.

My father wandered past the couch, saw the book open, walked out.

We're just pretending, I told him.

My mother was taking her finger on a tour of Italy. I just know I would love Italy, she was saying.

Where are *we*? I asked. Daddy, I called again, we're finding us now.

He was in their bedroom. That's good, he said, voice small through the hallway.

My mother thumbed to the table of contents. Page 45, she said, opening up. She skated her index finger down the gloss of the page, gliding past town names, a riverbed far away, searching, skiing, until her nail rested, clear, over a nest of pink and green lines and a black dot. Here, she said.

I peered down. There, I said. We're in that dot, I said.

We both bent close to the page, heads touching. I see you, I told her.

I'm winking, she said. Look closer. She even tilted her head to the ceiling and winked at it and I laughed, breathing in the smell of her shoulder—dish soap and almond moisturizer.

We looked up my aunt's home state, Colorado, and we looked up India and imagined all the people there. Millions, I said, finger on Calcutta, there are *millions* of people inside this dot. We looked at Kenya and pictured giraffes, sleeping. We looked at New Zealand and imagined sheep, chewing. After Peru, my mother closed the book.

I'm tired now, she said. Enough of that.

She handed the atlas over and I held it close; it was so big and broad I could barely get my arms around the whole thing. Maybe, I said, if I shake it—

She looked at me, standing, ready to go away. Good night Mona Blue, she said, leaving her palm on my head for one second.

I pushed up against it. If I shake it just right, I said, maybe we'll fall to the next page.

She smiled, kind of sadly.

Shake hard, she told me.

Removing her hand, she left the room and went to bed. I rattled the atlas like it was a bottle of juice, separated into water and pulp; I integrated that atlas. I shook hard, counted to ten, and opened to 45. Then turned the page to 46. Which put us in Australia.

Just like that! I said, out loud, to the quiet house. I put my finger smack in the middle of the continent, pinning it down.

People only notice if you leave; they don't notice if you stay. It's like hearing a buzz only after it's been turned off. My family spent every minute of every day in town and my father turned daylight on constellations of itchy red dots and his face was the color of wet worms and we told no one that anything was wrong. No one asked, either. I had instructions if they did. About a month or so after the first sick scare, my parents had specifically sat me down and asked me to please keep this between us.

I'd said: Keep what? What is *this*? What do you mean when you say *THIS*?

But my father had just coughed. My mother thumbed through a magazine. There was no name to say. The dictionary was not helpful. The encyclopedia was useless. Under *gray* in the thesaurus, all it said was *drab*. Under *gray* in the doctor's reference book, all it said was *Gray's Anatomy, excellent resource text*. Under *gray* in the phone book, all it said was us.

I went to my room and thought their plan of privacy was absurd and would never work but I found out fast that I was wrong. No one ever asked my father if anything was the matter. No one asked about his foggy pallor and no one came over with a casserole. No one took me under their wing to say, Mona are you okay? or talk about me in nice sad voices behind my back. Our fake-out was totally convincing.

Welcome back to school. My summer vacation was fine.

Which is why, when Lisa ran out of my classroom that Friday with the big I.V. crown on her head, before I went to recess duty, I had to go stand in a bathroom stall by myself. I stood, trembling inside the four small walls, because Lisa was so proud with the truth, she was a billboard and a megaphone, she'd made jewelry of saline and plastic, and I was thickly, fiercely, jealous.

6

The science teacher had moved here from a different state, one with big lakes and factories. He was new at the school too. We were the two new teachers. Apparently science teachers were equally hard to find—he was the son of the boss's college roommate, and he'd assembled all the factory items he could stand, and then drove out of his city in a truck. His name was Mr. Smith, but he didn't look like a Mr. Smith—it was an interesting name for him since his features were un-Smithlike, large and drooping, the features of harsh winters and heavy-duty politics.

He got in trouble right away, because he did an experiment where he split his groups of students and told half the class to talk to their houseplants kindly and the other half to talk to them abusively, cussing and insulting the plant, to see if tone and content made any difference in levels of growth. The kids assigned to cuss were thrilled beyond belief until Mimi Lunelle's mother found her daughter telling the bathroom fern it was a shame on the family's name and to fucking go to bed thirsty. Where did you learn to speak like that?! she demanded, horrified, and Mimi shrugged and then flicked the feathery leaves of the fern hard with her fingernails. Bitch, she said to the roots. She was sent straight to bed. Mrs. Lunelle called up the big boss. The science teacher was talked to, at length—first by boss, then by parents—and the experiment was halted. He was relegated to simpler projects involving salt crystals and build-your-own-atom kits.

I figured he was the school's problem teacher. I myself had had an excellent first week of teaching. I had it down. I was queen and countess. I was turning twenty in a week, and at nineteen felt I was the winner of the worldwide teaching contest, secretly judged behind closet doors and one-way mirrors.

The beginning of my unraveling started with that science teacher, on a Friday afternoon. Earlier in the day had been the first tricky Numbers and Materials we'd had so far, beginning with Elmer Gravlaki crawling out from under the table right before the bell rang with a 12 made of wood sitting atop the palm of his hand. It was cut perfectly to shape.

When do I go? he asked.

End of class, I told him. Hang on.

After drills and workbooks, I called Elmer to the front. He was fidgety, but held his wooden 12 up high, running his hand over the slope of the 2.

My dad is the address maker here, he said. He makes addresses. Elmer brought the 12 down to chest level. Nobody lives at this address, he said.

The class watched. $12 - 0 = 12$, he said. $12 - 1 = 11$.

Danny shot a rubber band at Elmer.

Stop, Danny, I said.

What? he said, eyes dewy brown at me. Danny had a big-time pushover mother.

Up front, Elmer's eyes were watering. $12 - 3 = 9$, he quivered.

Danny threw a button at his head. I was about to put Danny's name up on the board when Elmer, voice wavering like a teakettle, said: Danny, stop. I know where you live.

Danny's forehead raised. You do not, he said. Elmer, clutching his 12, swallowed and came out with 144 Main Street. The wood 12 was tottering in his palm, but Danny, who had a paper clip all set to throw, suddenly put it down, hearing those numbers (apparently the right ones) that marked where he slept every night. I was impressed. This was a fine armor for Elmer.

Well, where do YOU live? Ann DiLanno asked Elmer.

We're unlisted, he said, rubbing his palm over the 1.

Squirming up at the chalkboard, he did a few more and then sat, standing the number on his desk so it looked like he lived there. I knocked on it when I walked by, and Elmer smiled happily, as if I were knocking on the door to his unlisted house. Little did he know.

His presentation went very fast. Lisa said good job. He blushed, and then Ann DiLanno said she had one too.

Okay, I said, well, I guess we can have two today since Elmer's was so quick.

Ann stood up, smiling kind of meanly, and walked to the chalkboard.

Here, she said, throwing out her hands. A 3.

The class was looking around, at her fingers, at the floor.

I see no 3, said Lisa.

It's a 3 made of nothing, Ann said.

Oh that doesn't COUNT, said Elmer. I can do more with my 12, he said, suddenly brave now that he was done.

Nothing is a material, Ann said.

Sort of, I said. Try again. You can go next week, Ann. Look around your house for something that looks like a number. Be creative! I said.

I'm going next week, said Mimi Lunelle.

Hey Elmer, said Lisa, where do I live?

Look, Ann said, $3 - 3 = 0$. Ta da! It's magic. She twirled her ponytail with her index finger.

Lisa and Danny said, There's nothing there! and Ann was nodding smugly, and then they were out of their desks, ready to go feel her 3 of air or break it, and someone shoved someone and I had to write three names on the board. Waited to put check marks. Two check marks meant you would have to sit out at recess, on a bench, for fifteen minutes. Ann sat, and keeping her voice flat said it counted, it was a number and a material. She told Lisa to stop staring at her. I'm staring at nothing, Lisa said.

The bell rang and most of the class ran out.

Elmer lovingly packed up his 12. He turned to Lisa. You live at the hospital, he said.

I cleaned up my room during recess and taught my next classes, head full of thoughts about how to get Ann interested in Numbers and Materials. I stayed later than usual, stacking workbooks, but when I stepped out of my classroom to leave, I nearly tripped over John Beeze, in a ball on the hall floor, rolling back and forth and moaning.

Ooohh, he said.

John, I said, hey, are you all right?

He made a groaning sound.

I knelt down. What's wrong? I asked. Oh, you don't look

too good. Is your mom at the butcher shop? Let me go call her right now.

He groaned again and then whimpered in a reedy voice, No don't, he said, I'm fine, he said.

I put a hand on his forehead; he felt warm. John Beeze was rarely sick and was the kind of kid who fell ten feet from a swinging swing onto cement, stood up after one second, and ran across grass to flip over the slide.

I'm calling your mom, I said.

He clung to my sleeve. Don't, he said. It's scurvy, he said.

I blinked. What?

Scurvy, he whispered again. His eyes were half-shut and his cheeks were reddening.

You don't have scurvy, I said. I took my hand off his forehead. Only sailors get scurvy, I said. Who told you scurvy?

He watched me with big wet eyes and I saw a tear slide sideways down his cheek, cutting a line lighter than his skin tone down to his ear.

I stood. I'll be right back, I said, I'll just get her on the phone and she can take you to the doctor today.

He clung to my leg but I unpicked myself and headed to the kitchen area where the phone was. I'd never seen John like this and was thinking wash your hands, wash your hands, when I tripped over Ann DiLanno.

She was curled up in a ball too, on her side, breathing in shallow gasps.

Epidemic.

Ann, I said, what is going on? Are you okay?

Ms. Gray, she said, oooohhh.

I felt her forehead too. She, in contrast, felt all too cool.

Stay here, I said, don't move, I'll call your mother too. Go ask the art teacher for some water; drink water. Drink fluids.

I have croup, she said, rasping low.

You're delirious, I said. Don't move.

I wondered now if Ann had done that 3-of-nothing in a fit of fever, and I was feeling bad for criticizing her, and I was almost at the kitchen when I spotted two more: Elmer and Danny, flapping their bodies back and forth, heads lolling, necks too loose.

I ran into the kitchen to the phone and dialed information as fast as I could.

What city please? the operator asked.

It's all the same town, I spat, and you know it.

She coughed. Pardon me, she said. What number please?

I said this needed to be fast and I wanted to be connected right away right now to Mrs. Eudora Beeze, at the butcher shop. Inside the kitchen, the art teacher was washing brushes in the sink from her last art class, and that science teacher with the steady back and speckled arms was stooping down, speaking softly to Ellen, the best-behaved kid in the entire school.

They're all sick, I said, shrill, to the art teacher. Something is catching.

She didn't hear me over the faucet. As the line connected to the butcher shop, I concentrated hard on not touching my face and spreading this thing to myself. The phone rang two times.

Ring.

Ring.

A voice picked up. Hello?

I was thinking hot water, germs, meningitis, and my eyes grazed over the science teacher, who was wearing a bright red shirt that made me feel warm, but my ears focused and this time I picked up his conversation with Ellen. I'll keep my word, he was saying, and I promise you can do scurvy next week if you do a really good consumption today.

Hello? the voice on the phone said again. Butchery. Anyone there?

I pushed the receiver hard against my cheek. Ellen was nodding. What are my symptoms again? she asked. She leaned on the side of her foot.

He held her hands in his. Fatigue, he said, fatigue and a cough. Got it? Now . . . go!

Is anyone there? John's mother asked again, loud, too close to my ear where I was pressing down the plastic.

I hung up.

What is going on? I said mildly, pointing. The words were difficult to pronounce. The art teacher, scrubbing, didn't react. The science teacher was smiling at Ellen, who was walking out of the kitchen and smiling back. I walked over and tapped the art teacher on the shoulder.

She turned. Hey Mona, she said. She had green paint on her chin. I repeated my question. My voice was higher than usual.

You didn't know he had a background in theater did you? she asked. She beamed at the science teacher. We're so lucky, she said, that you're so multitalented.

In the background, outside the kitchen, I could hear Ellen, the notoriously obedient Ellen, begin to cough.

I backed out the door and peered into the hallway. John was still fetal on the ground. Ann was writhing. Ann had no problem going full-out for this teacher.

My lips tightened into wires. I faced Mr. Smith.

You. Are. Fired., I said.

Hey, aren't you done for the day? he asked. He raised up from his heels and pushed the hair out of his eyes with his wrist.

The art teacher pointed at me with a wet brush. By the way, she said, I think you guys live on the same block. Isn't this the coolest way to teach science? What's it called again?

Life Acting, he said. It helps them understand the symptoms for our Health segment. It's hands-on. Where do you live again?

He's *fired*, I said.

You can't do that, he said, laughing, actor, jovial, funny, ha-ha, ho-ho. You're not the boss. You're as new as me, he said. He scratched the back of his burn-marked hand. I did not smile. He looked me straight in the eye. I'm not fired, he said.

I actually spit on the floor. They stared at me, then at it, my spit, a pearl brooch starting to disintegrate on the tile. The art teacher giggled. I backed out of the room. The taste in my mouth was so bad I wanted to spit until I filled a bucket. A dirty pail, toxic, that would kill people.

In the big room, more kids were now strewn over the floor, like miniature Civil War soldiers.

Stand up! I called out, clapping my hands. Now! Science theater stupid class is over! Let's go!

The four I could see jumped to their feet immediately. I could hear the art teacher still giggling in the kitchen.

Ten laps around the floor, I called out. Stick to the wall. Then twenty push-ups.

They groaned.

Ellen is in charge, I said. She will make sure you do TEN laps. Now, GO, I said.

Their Velcro-tie sneakers began a steady plod around the circumference of the room.

Danny, stay close to the *wall*, I called again. John, that's your job. Keep them close to the wall.

Okay Ms. Gray! John piped in, legs moving twice as fast as anyone else's.

I opened the doors of classrooms, looking for extra fetal-balled children. The handwriting teacher, in the middle of a difficult lesson on cursive *G*, gave me a nasty look, but I ignored her.

I discovered one on the floor of my math room and one wilting against the wall of the spelling room; I assigned both laps. I kept looking, eyes burning, and finally, in the empty science room with Saturn mobiles turning very slowly from the ceiling, bingo, I found Lisa Venus curled in a ball underneath a table.

Uhhh, she groaned. Ow.

I walked over to her.

Get up, Lisa, I said. You are *not* sick.

Uhhh, she said again.

Now, I said. NOW.

She held herself up limply on her elbows. I can't, she said. I feel awful.

Get up! I yelled it.

She pulled to a sitting position. You're mean, she said.

You're healthy, I said back.

She blinked. At night, she said, I pretend I'm dead.

I bent halfway and stared at her underneath the flesh-toned table. Come on, Lisa, I said. All the way up. I don't want to have to put your name on the board again.

I have cancer, she said. She dropped back down and curled into an even tighter ball. Uhhh, she said. My side hurts.

I felt like evaporating, poof, I'm gone. I'm done. Of course she had cancer. Of course.

Did he assign you that? I asked, voice raising again, high. Did he do that?

No no, she said. I asked for it special.

I dropped down on my heels and touched her clump of hair.

My mom has cancer, she said.

I remember, I said, you told me. Eye cancer. That's very hard, I said. I thought you didn't even get colds.

She wears a red wig, Lisa said. It's real hair.

She flopped her hands loose on her wrists, like fish.

And I don't get colds, she said. This is acting class.

Lisa. I kept my hand on her small head. Why would you ask for cancer?

She rolled out slightly, so that she was on her back, facing the ceiling. I like it, she said. See, this way later, she said, when we watch TV? I can keep her company, she said.

I sank off my heels and sat down completely. I kept stroking down the bumps of her hair. We could hear the thumping of the kids running laps outside the science classroom door and Ellen's high voice, calling out: No, that's only eight! We have two more! I made a mental note to give Ellen a sticker.

My mom's wig is really red, Lisa said.

I know, I said.

You knew it was a wig? Lisa asked. She pulled in her knees and hugged them high up, heels nearly kicking her stomach.

No, I said. You told me.

It's made of human hair, she said. They had ones that weren't human hair but you could tell. My mom said it's worth the money to get real human hair.

C'mon, I said, Come on, Lisa. Please. Acting class is over.

Hang on, she said. I have a little more cancer to do. She squeezed her eyes shut.

I sat and watched her. She rolled back and forth, scrunching up her eyes, and after two more minutes, sat up.

Okay, she said, I'm done.

She stood and gave me a spontaneous hug.

You know my dad is sick too, I said to her then.

Her face opened with interest, and she hopped from foot to foot.

Does he have eye cancer? Lisa asked, ready to drop down again and roll around some more.

No, I said, not cancer at all.

What does he have? She edged toward the door. Outside, her classmates had stopped running and were laughing about something.

I don't know, I told her. It doesn't have a name.

She nodded before she bolted away. Oh yeah, she said. I think I've heard of that.

7

That evening, I called the boss to tell her what the science teacher was doing.

Oh I *know*, she said. Isn't it interesting.

I walked to my bed. No, I said, knuckles rubbing splinters off the potted tree trunk. I find it entirely uninteresting, I said.

She cleared her throat. Anything else? she asked. How's math going?

A whole lot of people died of scurvy, I said. Tomorrow morning when you drink your orange juice—

She wished me a good night, then hung up. I knocked so hard on the potted tree, I knocked it over.

Sunday marked my twentieth birthday, and my mother called me early in the morning, singing half the song before she got bored and cut herself off. Then she said: Okay you big 20, let's go out for breakfast for once. Like a family, she said. I pulled myself up in bed. We are a family, I told her groggily, wrapping the blankets closer around me. Her voice was solid in my ear. Well, like another family then, she said.

I took a shower with my eyes closed. I'd slept bad all weekend, knocking forever before I could sleep, pushing every disease I could name into the wood: scurvy, croup, cholera, polio, mumps, scabies, bubonic plague, eye cancer—get away from my hand, get into the roots, get out of the blood like bad water.

As I dried off, I played the one message on my machine, which was from the art teacher, wishing me a good one; she was the kind who noted birthdays down in her little book with the vigor of someone who has often been forgotten. She made no reference to the firing and spitting episode on Friday. I put on a dress with dark grassy patterns on it, and at my parents' house, my mother held my hands out in hers and said I looked lovely. I blushed, her bashful suitor. My father was in a bad mood; he said, Happy birthday, but then muttered how earlier that morning, he'd gotten a sunburn from watering the grass, and his skin was prickly and hot.

We drove the six blocks over and parked. The coffee shop turned out to be packed because this was the Sunday of the annual fall marathon and lots of people were out and about. A troop of runners passed, leg muscles taut and curved in the back of the thigh, and a cheer went up from the sidewalk.

After ten minutes, the host called our name and we sat down.

The booth by the door was drafty. The booth in the back was dirty. The booth in the middle was right under the air conditioner.

It's cold, said my father. His face was small.

I wanted to go home and go away.

My mother was steady and firm. She liked to make these situations the best possible for my father so that he would come back for the next birthday. She waved down the waiter and had him turn down the air conditioner, although he himself was sweaty from work. She asked for hot tea. I drank my juice and thought of dead bodies on big ships, how one sip of this powdered mix from concentrate in its small bumpy diner glass might've straightened their spines, revived them in minutes, eyes blinking and new with miraculous C.

We ordered and talked but the whole meal was spent checking on my father, who was shivering inside a mysterious chill that neither my mother nor I could feel. She tasted the tea for him, like a courtier testing the food of the king for poison, and she, zealous courtier, thought the lemon tasted funny. We sent it back. They brought a second pot of tea, with no lemon at all. My mother said this one was not very hot. I shrank in the booth, my dress a receding meadow.

More marathon people clapped by outside. The morning was dry and I knew just how the sweat felt on their skin, air crackling in the nostrils like popcorn. I hated being near running events with my father: he used to run; I used to run.

At the end of the meal, my father remembered he needed plant food for the backyard from the hardware store. I leapt at the chance; my pancakes were done and I needed to get out of there.

My father pulled a twenty from his wallet. That's a big help Mona, he said. Thanks. Get a good kind, he said. Ask Jones what works.

I hadn't set foot in the hardware store in years.

My mother pulled a fifty from her wallet. For your birthday, she said. Buy yourself something good. Just promise me you won't put it in the bank.

The bank is closed, I said.

All the better, said my mother. She turned to my father. Since when do you garden? she asked.

I'll meet you at home, I said, standing, leaving them with their cooling tea and irritable waiter. Outside, the air was warm and the streets bright with orange cones, but lucky for me, there was no sign of runners anywhere.

The sprinklers turned on in the park, shush. I was jittery from the breakfast, so as I walked down the block, I considered my new number 20. XX. Twenty is a score. An icosahedron has twenty faces. The sum of some of its own factors: 1, 4, 5, 10. The wholeness of that zero, the brand-spanking-new two. Welcome to the next decade.

I passed the movie theater and the bank. I walked by the bookstore, the post office, the drugstore, the candy shop, all the way to the very end of the block, to the brick and glass building that housed the one and only hardware store in town. When I pushed open the glass door, stomach jerking, and entered, the store was empty of customers. Which felt surprisingly right. These minutes were mine.

The bells rang my entrance but everything else was quiet except for the rustle of a newspaper turning at the counter. Mr. Jones was perched on a stool at the cash register, wearing green, reading. He barely glanced up. I barely glanced at him. I saw the familiar lump underneath his shirt, but I didn't feel like asking him what it was. Instead, I drifted down Aisle One. Here were screens, faucets, outlets, hinges—everything you forget isn't just organically part of a house. I picked up a doorknob of blue glass and twisted it in the air. Open. I could hear Mr. Jones flutter his paper at the counter.

I had said something about his number necklaces for the first time when I was nine. It'd been one of his months of 2, a very bad time, and for a while I'd just watched as he took out the trash with that wax 2 around his neck, then trundled back inside his house, head low and silent. I petted his hedges with my hand, hoping to make him somehow feel better. I hadn't seen him for a few days and was getting increasingly worried when one afternoon, as I was riding my bike around the block, Mr. Jones came outside with his car keys jingling, wearing an 18.

Hi Mr. Jones! I'd said, riding down the sidewalk toward him, eager.

Hey there Mona, he said.

I'm glad you're feeling better, I said. Nine times better.

He stopped opening his car. I rode closer. His face looked soft and worn as cloth.

Why thank you, he said. That's truly nice of you to notice, he said. That's a nice thing to do, for a kid to notice that.

Well, I said. 18 is nine times higher than 2. That's a ton higher.

He winked at me. Still, he said. You'd be surprised at how many people never say a word.

He wished me a good day and then got in his car and drove off. All afternoon I felt great, having noticed. I was a good noticer. So I noticed everything that day—I overnoticed. I told another neighbor walking around that I liked her new haircut and she hugged me. I told the little boy who played up the street that he had a bleeding arm and he said, What? and ran off, scared. It stopped when I told my dad he looked tired and my mom said that was rude and to go clean my room.

The following year was when my father dropped out of the active world, and it was that same year that my feelings changed for Mr. Jones. At age thirteen, I often found myself spitting on that hedge that separated our house from his, and one Halloween, I egged his garage, by myself, with two dozen eggs, a few of which were rotten.

He never found out it was me. He wore a 10 all that week, picking the shells painstakingly from his driveway with a handheld broom and trash receptacle.

A few months later, he dropped down to 3. I didn't say a word about it. I was waiting by the car one morning for my mother to drive me to school when Mr. Jones came through his front door to take out his trash. It was not yet eight A.M., and the air was cold and pale.

Oh hi Mr. Jones, I said.

I thought I caught him looking at me mournfully, and I figured he was thinking I was a self-absorbed teenager now and had lost my youthful candor and observation skills. But I was standing there, completely aware of the loud and sad 3 around his neck, just refusing to comment.

Hi Mona, he said, voice hopeful.

So, I said, playing it up. So Mr. Jones, why do you wear those numbers around your neck like that?

His eyebrows bunched in, like a dog's.

I thought you knew, he said.

I stared straight at him, eyes cold with hate; I was thinking about how for three years straight now, Mr. Jones had seen my father get into his car in his suit of triple shades of gray and his face with its weird fogged absent skin and how he'd never said a single thing. No one else did either, but I thought Mr. Jones, the man who praised noticers, might. I was wearing an invisible sign of my own now. It said: Up Yours Hypocrite.

Never once did he look at me and say: Mona, I know something is going on, and I notice you look sadder than you used to.

It would've meant a million dollars to me if he'd said something like that. I would've been his slave forever. Instead, he kept changing his numbers and going about his day and lifting and lowering like a teeter-totter.

Don't you remember? he asked that morning, approaching the hedge.

I blinked slowly. Remember? I said, hard. Remember what?

He stared at me, disbelieving, and then went back inside for a minute, and came out again wearing a 1. The number hung heavy around his neck as he finished taking out the trash. He didn't look at me again. I'd never seen the 1 before; it was very new-looking. I had a horrible day at school and when the substitute math teacher asked me to do the equation, I nailed it, found the value of y, and then said I had to go to the nurse, couldn't she see I was in the midst of choking?

8

Mr. Jones was still lost in the height of his newspaper as I turned the corner and drifted down Aisle Two. Here were screwdrivers, dead bolts, rows of hammers. I squeaked the shiny purple plastic of a shower curtain, and stroked the maple handle of a saw. The truth is, I love hardware stores. I longed to fill my arms with all of it, run back to the diner, and thrust a metal bouquet at my chilled father, consisting of wrench, pliers, and drill.

Yell: Go! Fix yourself!

I pictured them walking back to the car by now, slow, the sunburn a ruddy murky swamp drowning away my father's face.

On the front wall of the hardware store, all seven different clocks clicked to five-to-eleven. I wandered down Aisle Three. This row smelled sharp with cedar, and contained nuts and bolts, can openers, wooden spoons. Mallets and glue guns. Knives with sharp blades, my profile elongated, eyes slivered and blue in the silver.

Across the street, someone let out a loud hoot about one of the runners. I touched each knife and turned the corner.

Aisle Four had the gardening supplies. Hoses and shovels and hand-drawn signs that marked the placement of fruits and vegetables. I saw a few of Elmer Gravlaki's father's addresses hanging on the wall for sale, ornate wooden 2s and 17s, sanded to the smoothness of pebbles, and thought of Elmer, walking around with everyone's house number rolling around in his head, the same way another kid learns to make his fist harder.

Closing in three minutes! called out Mr. Jones from his stool.

Closing? I said. It's barely eleven in the morning.

He didn't answer.

I found plant food in a green package nestled next to a pointy spade. I'd never seen my father garden but it seemed like a fine activity for a faded person, and this plant food looked as good as the one in the blue package and the one in the red package and who really needed to ask Mr. Jones anything. Half my job was done. In Aisle Five, I picked up a handful of nails, cold little metal fence posts, and stirred them in my palm. I was trying to think of how to explain to my mother that I'd broken my promise, shown up empty-handed, started a new tradition of no presents at all, when right then, two minutes before closing, I turned my head one inch to the left, and saw what I wanted for my twentieth birthday.

My heart picked up a beat. I knew it instantly, dripped the nails back into their bin, and walked over.

There was only one left.

Hanging from a hook high on the wall, in Aisle Five, was a medium-sized solid steel ax. Sharp and mean and perfect. I didn't know if I had ever actually seen an ax before, but this particular model was the basic type you read about woodcutters using, with a flared silver blade attached to a light grainy wooden handle the color of unsunned blond hair.

Everyone makes fun of shopping but it's all about this. It's all about suddenly attaching to an object so deeply you can't leave it in the store. I wanted that ax. I was meant for that ax. I loved the graceful skirt of the blade and how it looked like it came all the way from a forest. I loved how the edge was so sharp it glittered, and the powerful way the metal poised like a panther on the wood. It was such a hopeful ax, up there, wanting to be bought and used, in this warm-weather town where the houses were built without chimneys. I reached up and lifted it off the wall and brought it straightaway to Mr. Jones. The sudden flush of birthday prickled over the back of my neck.

Just in time, I said.

He looked up from his newspaper and checked the price tag.

Twenty-four dollars, he said.

It's my birthday, I told him.

He folded the paper into fourths and put it to the side. Unusual choice, he said. How old?

Twenty, I said.

He nodded. Lucky for both of us I'm still open, he said.

I'd like to buy this ax, I said. And some licorice.

He carefully removed the price tag from the stem of the ax and then pulled a rope of red licorice out of the bin near his knees.

Here, he said. That'll be nineteen dollars. I'll give you a twenty percent discount being that it's your birthday. Plus one dollar for the licorice. Twenty even. A dollar per year, he said, nodding at the sense of it.

I could smell the Sunday air drifting into his store, dry and vast, the moving sky.

Thanks, I said. I pulled the crumpled fifty from my pocket and handed it to Mr. Jones. Fifty: half a life, maybe. Half a countdown. L. I thought of telling my mother, voice somersaulting with glee, how for once I'd found something I really wanted. Her forehead would clear, face smooth; she'd say, How wonderful Mona! What did you get?

It's useful, I'd tell her. I'll use it.

Mr. Jones counted the change backward into my palm. I folded the bills and placed them in my back pocket together: one bill the new age I was right now; the other the age I was when my father turned from a robust man who raced me on the track to one who froze inside restaurants.

That's forty and fifty, Mr. Jones said, and—

I don't need a bag, I told him. I'll carry it. Oh, and the plant food too.

I'd almost forgotten the little sinking bag on the counter.

He rang that up.

What's a girl like you doing with an ax? he said. You going to chop firewood? He laughed at his own joke.

Don't you remember me? I asked him.

He scrunched up his nose. Remember you, he said. Remember what? That's four dollars.

Absentmindedly, I ran my index finger down the silver blade of the ax, and even though it had been hanging up high, unsharpened and ignored, the edge cut right through the skin. Blood blossomed forth, a rose.

Oh no, he said. Look at that. Let me get you a tissue.

It's okay, I said. I gave him a ten, backing away. I used to live next door to you, I said. Mona Gray. Left side. You remember that, right? I was your math student, I said. Your star pupil.

He handed over the change and looked at me, reaching for a tissue, half off his stool.

What are you planning to do with that ax? he said.

What's your number today, Mr. Jones? I asked.

He blinked, surprised. I took another step back and he reached beneath his shirt, obedient, and through the collar pulled out a small precise 12, made of wax, about the size of a tennis ball, hanging on a string and gleaming dully in the lamplight.

12, I said.

12, he said. Thanks for asking.

Not so great, I said.

No, he said, not especially.

His face had opened up now, since I'd asked to see it, clean, wide, as if I'd turned a key and walked directly into his body.

But I did the opposite instead—backed away from him more, that eagerness in his face, edging toward the door. I could feel the sunlight behind me, waiting, the step into dryness. I bit off the end of the licorice rope.

He was off his stool now, staring at my finger, bleeding all over the blade. The 12 bounced around his neck but I was out of the store, entrance bell singing my exit; outside, the light was white and the park sprinklers had been turned off, leaving fleeting tiaras of dew on the air.

Coiling the licorice around my wrist, I held the plant food in one hand and the ax high and blinding in the other. The stem waggled in my grip.

Will you look at this! I said out loud to the world. Just what I've always wanted! I said.

9

In the street, two orange cones had tipped over, vivid and isosceles. The coffee shop was still crowded with people. My parents' car was gone.

I used the ax first to circle the air around my head, then to brush against the bark of trees, then to lean on like a walking stick. I loved my new present, but I didn't like being around marathons, and I didn't like that Mr. Jones hadn't remembered me, and I wasn't sure how to manage going to school in the morning with kids who would cough at will and like it. I did the walk to my parents' house slowly, eating licorice, sucking on my bloody finger, passing abandoned folding chairs set up by the side of the road. Families stood outside on their lawns, talking, drinking iced tea. It was just past eleven o'clock. The streets were calm with Sunday.

I walked by the flowery house where John Beeze lived with his mother, the butcher, and the green public house that no one could stay in because the pipes were damaged by a root. Kids liked to play there when it was raining. More than one town member had been conceived in its back rooms.

Bikes lay flat on lawns, wheels spinning.

The plant food sifted and shifted in my hand, and I leaned on the ax, blade lilting out like a song, and debated where to put it once I got home. Bedroom? Windowpane? Closet? Someone let out another sports yell, several blocks away.

I rounded the corner. I was now about seven houses from where my parents lived.

All these homes I knew very well. I had known all my neighbors growing up. Mr. Jones still lived on my parents' right side, but on the left had lived an old woman named Mrs. Finch. For years she baked terrible cakes and brought them to her neighbors on birthdays, never missing a year, waiting at the door while we took a bite and nodded and smiled over the awful sour salt glob in our mouths.

I approached her house, balancing that ax head on my shoe.

Mrs. Finch was important to me. Not because I knew her that well, or because of the cakes, which were awful. She'd stopped baking in her later years, and become a sickly lady with a cane, a walker, and a wheelchair, all three, so it wasn't a huge surprise to anyone when she died. I was twelve then, and two of my grandparents had died by that point so I wasn't totally unfamiliar with death, particularly the deaths of old people.

The remarkable thing had happened the day *before* she died. I had been riding past her house on my bike, back and forth on the sidewalk, too scared to dip into the street and head downtown. I stayed on the sidewalk even though people on foot gave me dirty looks. Whenever I rode my bike, I felt one second away from flying over the handlebars: dizzy, then dizzier, then dead.

As I rode by, I spied on Mrs. Finch's lawn a piece of butcher paper wrapped around her front-lawn tree, and written on the butcher paper had been a number, in black block ink. The number was 84. I remember looking at it and wondering why her address was so much shorter than ours, and why she'd stuck it on her tree, or if Mr. Jones had put it there in a really good mood, and then I decided that it wasn't her address or Mr. Jones at all, and spent a good minute or so thinking about that, why was it there? rambling along in my own head, pedaling down, knocking on tree trunks, thinking thoughts I never would have thought of again, thoughts meant to be unremembered, if it hadn't been that she died the next week and in the obituary it said she was 84 years old.

I looked at that typeface on the newspaper and the butcher paper number lit up in my head.

There was a beauty and an order that I liked. I found it peculiar, but I also found it perfect.

I tore that obituary out of the newspaper, and saved it. I placed it in the drawer of my wood nightstand set aside for unusual items, where it shared space with a tiny plastic running man, a gum wrapper in Spanish, and the one warped page of my aunt's lingerie catalog that I hadn't been able to throw out.

Birthdays passed and no one got a sour salt cake anymore. I forgot all about the 84 until the whole thing happened again, and this time it was much worse.

Across from Mrs. Finch was a big friendly yellow house. Right now someone else lived there, some family with eleven cats, but when I was growing up, that was where the Stuarts lived. They were really nice, tall people, even though they didn't like the horn on my bike and got irritable when once on an impulse I picked one of their prime golden roses for my hair. They'd had three kids around my age, and a new one, a brand-new baby, pink and fleshy on the blanket, with curling fingers.

I was thirteen years old, biking up the sidewalk one afternoon, when I saw a flag flying on the Stuarts' lawn. It was a flag with a circle on it, one big black o. I remember supposing they were some weird religion that worshipped o's. I spent a good minute thinking about them, about what that meant, about tires, about rings, about lunar eclipse.

I had a flash of worry before I went to sleep, but so swift I never would've remembered that either.

A week later, their baby died. It was in its crib and Mrs. Stuart left the room and when she came back the baby wasn't breathing anymore. Just like that. She brought it into the world; it took off. Didn't like it. Left. Mrs. Stuart shook it many times, she apparently never really GOT it; she just stared and questioned, asked questions to the baby: Are you okay? What is going on? Baby? She was nothing but question marks and she couldn't grasp it, but I did; I got it. I remembered the o.

Could I have warned them? What to say? I quit riding my bike and retired it to the side wall of the garage. Cars lined up in front of the Stuarts' house and people walked to their door, hugging casserole dishes close to the heart, food warm through the glass, dampening their shirts. The o flag flipped and waved in my head. I did not know how to make a casserole and I never spoke with the Stuarts again. I did, however, bring them a replacement rose, for the one I'd clipped months before; I bought a long-stemmed red at the store and stuck it, like a pole, next to their rosebush. A sentry rose. To watch out for pickers. After a few months, the Stuarts and their three alive children moved away, I think to Florida.

Some worries sit in the stomach like old bad food. Most of the time, they are so quiet and dormant you can't feel them at all. Oh good, you might think. They're gone.

The fall marathon was held only once a year on the Sunday of the last week of September. This Sunday—of my birthday, of plant food, of axes, of breakfast. The race went through all the neighborhoods, and the small group of local runners spent months training to loop the town. Brief synthetic shorts, heavily muscled thighs. Shoes soft as slippers.

No one I knew ever ran in the marathon. I didn't set up a folding chair to watch it because I couldn't stand seeing those people running, the shapes of muscles moving inside their legs like activated geometry. I didn't like to think about winning it which is always the only thing I thought about when I watched.

I was twirling the ax handle, walking by Mrs. Finch's house, walking by the Stuarts' old house, passing folding chair after folding chair, when I reached my destination and saw, edges lifting in the wind, a marathon identification number resting lightly on my parents' front lawn.

And it said 50.

I looked at the paper on the lawn.

It said 50, there was no doubt, it was the number-fifty runner. Black number on white paper, bordered with orange.

I wasn't on my bike this time. If I tried to sit on that bike, my feet would drag on the cement. I walked over to the paper and picked it up. It was made of that unrippable kind of fabric—not paper, not cloth; it was made of some toxic material created in a factory in a different country, sent over in boxes on a big metal boat.

My mother was older than my father. In July, she had turned 53. His birthday was in a month.

I ran my fingers over the numbers; they were thick, and dark, and certain. 50.

I used to think death might be hidden somewhere on our bodies. Tucked behind the pupil like a coin, slid beneath the thumbnail, ribbon-wrapped around a wrist bone. A sharp, dark sliver; a loose, pale pellet. Each person different. Each lifespan set. On the day of your death, it melts out through your entire body, a warm, broken bath bead. Until then, it waits—sealed and silent. If you knew where to look, you could find it, resting in the curve of your ear, waiting patiently for its right day. Those people who survive brutal car accidents: not their day yet. Those people who die from one bad hamburger: their bead was up. I've always steered clear of fortune-tellers, because what if she was real and she found it? Slid it out from beneath your thumbnail, held it to the light, and told you.

On this day. On this hour. You have this much left.

I avoid fortune-tellers for two reasons. For one: what if she glanced at me and said: *Mona*, and her voice sank. Oh poor Mona. She can't disguise her pity. She says: You will die young, you will die a girl who has never found her place in the world. Your heart will quit you before its time.

I exit the tent, shoulders low, body crippling.

But below that lives the other fear, the less known fear, the rumbling flood: what if she said this. What if she said: Oh Mona, and her voice soared. Oh *Mona*, she said, you will live so long. You are going to have a life and it's going to be something beautiful.

This 50 was not for me; I lived elsewhere. It was not for my mother, she was already past.

I stood on the lawn and the leaves on the tree covering the kitchen window were blinking in the breeze and I could guess where he was inside. In front of the television, half-watching, taking note of everything living inside his skin. Gallbladder? Check.

Liver? Check. Heartbeat? Check. Brain? ABCDEFG . . . Check. He is aware of her, puttering around the house, throwing away junk mail without regret. (I'll never use this coupon, she announces. Carpet cleaning? Forget it. Trash. She is so good at throwing things out.)

I stood on the lawn with the paper fluttering at my feet and the tree fluttering over the kitchen window and the two people I loved most in the world separated from me by walls and years.

I didn't go in yet. I imagined the Stuarts in Florida. Kids almost grown by now. Tanned. Sidestroke champions. I think of the now-youngest Stuart, Joanna; she was ten when the baby died. She's with her first boyfriend, in his living room, and he has a new baby brother sleeping in a crib nearby. The boyfriend asks her: Do you like babies? And she says: Babies? Babies? I'm not sure. He doesn't ask anymore; he has fulfilled his questioning duties and now removes her shirt. While she feels her breast kissed for the first time in her life, something sweeter than an ache, a sharpened ache, a purified ache, she is thinking about that creamy movement inside the crib. It had been a girl. That had been her only sister. The youngest. She was supposed to outlive them all.

My eyes are closed but I see him inside: my father, 50, watches TV alone. If I listen very hard, I can hear those electric voices from the television wandering out the open window to reach me.

I don't move yet.

Somewhere across town, feet firm on the gravel, the fastest and steadiest person in town breaks the tape, and wins the marathon.

part two

50

10

My father was a track star in college. He showed me photos from his scrapbook once, of himself in a line with ten or so other men, each with knobby knees and thighs too exposed, the styles of uniform different then. The terrible vulnerability of his bare skin. The whole thing made me embarrassed to look at, but then he turned the pages and to my surprise there were all the prizes he'd won—blue ribbons, smushed behind plastic, forcing the pages of the scrapbook to lift too high. First place in sprint—fifty-yard dash. First place in relay—he was the anchor. First place in long jump. That one amazed me. Really? I asked, rereading the flakes of golden writing on the blue satin. He nodded. His hands, with their carefully shaped pale fingernails atop the page, looked to me now as though they had never moved fast through anything.

He encouraged me to do track, and before he got sick, we raced until the dust flew, and my lungs grew sharp with air and want. I ran again on the high school track team, but when I started doing really well, of course, I quit. I told my dad it just wasn't my thing—too competitive, is what I said. He'd nodded, but the track coach had been crushed. She tried to talk to me, but I just recited some well-used slogans: My schoolwork, I explained. She brandished my report card, miraculously, from her pocket. But you're getting A's! she said. I would rather focus on the other parts of my life, I said. She hung her head and spoke to the ground. There is practically nothing in the world as beautiful and simple as running, she said.

I couldn't stand to hear that, and left. I went to two track meets during the year, but all I saw were the mistakes everyone made and was filled with the intense desire to show off, so I stopped going. On high school graduation day, the coach came over to wish me well. She was wearing a dress and looked ridiculous.

Good luck to you Mona, she said, and hugged me.

I felt a vague sense of floating. Her hug was loose and light. Good luck to you too, I said.

She smiled, then leaned forward.

So why did you quit, really, she asked.

Behind us, hundreds of my peers in their green robes and green hats were hugging parents. I'd already hugged mine; my mother had held my face, proud, and my father had praised and beamed and then sat, exhausted.

I looked back to the coach. The yellow tassel of my hat bobbed near the corner of my eye like a building in the distance.

I quit because winning is lonely, I said.

Her face moved back slightly. Clearly, she'd expected some story about a boyfriend.

But if you ran for the joy of running—

I interrupted. Whatever, I said. My voice was flat now. I patted her shoulder.

Thanks for everything, I said, and I walked away.

The morning after I found the marathon 50, I woke up in my clothes, 4:30 bright on the clock, each number a house of slim red parallelograms. I felt inside my pocket and of course there it was, and I took it out and unfolded it and the numbers were clear, and panic bloomed in my stomach again, an ecstatic flower.

I got a warning. No one gets a warning.

I wanted to marry wood. I wanted to chew down some two-by-fours, crawl inside a tree, slide elm into my aorta so that every beat of every second was a grand waltz with luck.

I was awake and alert right away. Got up. Went to the kitchen. My shoes were on already. I'd slept all night wearing shoes. I opened the cabinet underneath the sink and took out the ax which I'd stored there as soon as I'd come home because at the time it seemed like as good a place as any to store an ax. The blade smelled like lemon-fresh detergent.

The handle slipped from the sweat in my palm but the ax winked in the darkness like a glint from a reptile's cornea and I sat on the living room couch with myself, in the dimness that comes before early morning, and wondered what was about to happen.

51: Humming, just around the corner.

On the lawn the day before, when I couldn't stand to stare at the 50 anymore, I'd folded it into my pocket, hid the ax in the bushes, and gone inside my parents' house. After choking down birthday cake with my mother, I watched TV with my father for hours. He said cake made him queasy, and sipped mineral water through a straw. He looked the same as always. My mother had wanted to know if I'd bought anything for myself at the hardware store and I said, No? with a question mark and she looked at me funny. I'll get something soon, I said. I need a shower curtain.

Before I walked home, she'd come out with me to the front lawn.

It was night by then, and the sky was crowded with stars, a geometric dream of pinpoints.

She said she remembered my birth. I said she should forget it by now. You, she said, touching my arm, you have so much ahead of you, I can just see it.

This felt vaguely like a threat. Bye, I said.

She stood under the front-lawn tree, and one white bloom drifted down the side of her face, a huge soft earring.

Mona, she said. She fixed her gaze right on me then, straight through the evening blueness, in such a direct way that I felt myself freeze, recede, loosen. I shook my head against it, reaching out a hand to touch the tree trunk. Between the bark and my mother's straight-on gaze, I felt some kind of shimmer in the air. I couldn't bear it.

Talk to you tomorrow, I said.

Once the door clicked, and I knew she was inside, I ran to the bushes and retrieved the ax, blade now cold from the night air. The handle was a rush of relief in my hand. I didn't need to touch any tree trunks with my palm pressed tight against that wood.

In my dark apartment, 4:40 in the morning, shaky from the absence of sleep, nothing made me calmer right then than holding that blond wooden handle and looking at that skirt of shining steel.

It felt right. It seemed possible, and useful: to join the troops.

I considered some options.

The easiest would be a finger or a toe. This was the most conservative choice. Fingers would be obvious but I could hide an absent toe, maybe my whole life. I never wear sandals.

But big deal. Too small an offer.

I could slice off a kneecap, that smooth moving skipping-stone of a bone, shine it up and use it as a paperweight, give it to my boss as a holiday gift for her already overcrowded boss desk.

I could cut off my heel. I could cut off my hand. I could cut off my arm. I could cut off more.

Ears. Eyes. Nose. Calves.

Shoulders. Legs. Breasts. Fists.

The ax was clean and bright and manly. There was a sick feeling in my stomach, this side of throwing up, but it had, within its center, the undeniable bubbling of excitement. I could change my life, right here. I could make myself different and I would be different that way for my whole life, forever, and this—right here—would be the moment where everything turned.

Blam. New me. In the newspapers. In the butcher shop. Read about by Mr. Jones on the stool in his hardware store. I bet you remember me now, that girl around town with no head on her shoulders.

I held the handle close. Silly Mona, I said, and I almost got up to put it away but I didn't move because I didn't want to. The ax felt so good in my hands, so strong and real, so regular and steady, and that 50 was loud and clear on my bed.

I gripped the sturdy wooden stem and got up off the couch, stretching flat on my back on the carpet. Staring at the ceiling, I brought the blade into the air. It was heavy, and as I looked at it winking, I thought of something to do. My heart clanged, and thrill and terror dribbled through me, giddy and light, and I pulled myself up and stood, almost burping up bubbles like bells.

Holding the ax high in my right hand, I imagined it first: my arm, swinging down, a loose curve, swing down, and crash, crack, I let the blade bury deep down wherever the swing ends. Sshh, quiet, woozy, dreamy, the girl falls, sshh, tipping over, falling, something has been hit, timber, she's over, there's a slice in her leg, I'm bleeding all over the carpet, but there's the towel! And there's my father! And when someone asks at the hospital of glass, when they're trying to cure my incurable wound, when they question me in high tones what happened, I say in a clear voice: I chopped myself down.

And then I'm the talk of the hospital for a while. It's my best stint with fame.

My arm was up, ax up, high up, imagining this girl as me, loving it, heady with the image: I'm limping to the hospital, leaving a trail of blood on the ground; I'm pausing at the entrance where the building flies up in front of me like long hard water; I'm in the elevator, I'm in a room, ready to sneak out, preparing my escape so I can limp to my parents' house and tell them I did it! I saved the family; my hair is fetchingly mussed and the hospital gown is billowing up like a wedding dress, and I am as noble as the rest of them and I am a part of the team, I am a team player, and then, of all things, in the middle of this, of all people, Lisa Venus popped into my head.

She's in the hospital too, lost, peering out a blue window at the dark blue night, looking for the other wing, both of us imprisoned by the masterful glass architecture. I have a chunk missing from my leg and maybe I don't have a foot—who knows—and she is walking through the halls, little Lisa, holding a drawing, and she's asking where the cancer ward is because that's where her mother lives.

And she sees me. Ms. Gray! she says. What are you doing here?

But I'm weak in the hospital bed without enough blood and I can't even sit up. You can tell she thinks I look bad without makeup. The hospital nurse comes to her side quickly because she doesn't want this little girl with the nice drawing of the skull and crossbones, she doesn't want this little girl to be talking to the nut who thinks she's a tree to cut down.

Ms. Gray, says Lisa, and her face is screwing up and she looks like she's about to erupt into tears.

In my apartment, I have my arm to the sky and the ax is waggling in it and I'm a statue here; I'm waiting to see if I'll do it. Will I do it. Will I mark myself.

In the hospital, I tell Lisa: Don't worry, I'm just here for a visit. In fact I'm right about to leave.

I try to get out of bed, but my head rushes from the weakness and the nurse has clamped a hand down on Lisa's shoulder and is guiding her away. I can hear her start to cry in the hallway. They're taking her to the cancer ward now. Everyone there is bald. Which is hard to see, that is hard too, but if you're bald, you don't have hair NOT to brush and so you don't look matted up, and crazy, and neglected, and old. You just look less.

I manage to get up out of the hospital bed, and holding on to the wall I trail Lisa in my hospital nightgown. The moon is shining through the glass, a dome of blue, making shadows the color of morning sky on the pale tiled floors. We go to see her mother. She is a sleeping skull against a thin white pillow.

Lisa is so bristlingly alive with everything, I feel like she has absorbed all the flourescence accidentally. She goes to the bed, and sits there on the edge of it. She puts her drawing on the side table, and starts to sing a song about kickball. Her mother still sleeps. I look down my side, through my hospital gown, and the gash is as thick and deep as it can be without severing something, and I try to move the skirt to hide it but hospital gowns tend to show a little leg. If she turned, she could see it. A piece of me: gone.

I wait for her to turn. I am waiting for her to turn. I am watching the back of her head, and waiting for her to find out.

You. Hey—. You're not what I thought.

Against the wall, I am doubling over. This is a bad feeling. I want to scoop up Lisa and take her to get ice cream in the cafeteria but I'm a one-legged lady with a crack in her shin and it's getting harder and harder to move.

Race me, she says, dashing off in a blur, and she laps the hall four times, cheeks red from exertion, alive! alive!, panting, done by the time it takes me to hobble to the doorway and watch her go. The look on her face when she sees how little I've come.

Inside my apartment, I put down the ax.

11

The morning was still dark when I left. Hauling the ax over my shoulder, I walked to the school, let myself in, and went straight into MATH. Flicked on the light. The room illuminated—dim, wrong. The cutout numbers were curling inside their frames. The chalkboard still had Friday's date on it.

Classrooms only look right in daylight. The whole place made me feel tired.

I searched in the cabinets until I found what I needed, then pulled an orange plastic chair to the wall, hammered some nails, and hung the ax up high. I hung it backward, blade to the left. When I was done, the room began to warm with light, and through the windows from the hall I could see the sky widening and opening, the first cars tooling down the streets. I sat in a chair and put my head on the desk and finished sleeping.

When the sun was up, the main doors flung open and a wallop of kids charged in, so full of energy they made my teeth ache. I got up and made myself a cup of tea, then headed in to see the kindergartners.

I forced myself to focus. We went over addresses and phone

numbers. The first graders added 4 and 5 and 1 together. No one said anything about the new decoration.

By third period, it was, naturally, Lisa Venus who noticed first. She saw it hanging on the wall within five seconds of entering the classroom.

I like the 7, she said, pointing up. I grinned, huge, at her.

What's that for? asked Mimi Lunelle, walking in wearing a pink dress with ribbons tied in bows all over it.

People sometimes use it to chop wood, I said, but we're going to use it as a 7.

Ann walked in the door and sat in her seat. She glowered, listening for a minute, then said, in her usual flat tone: That is a hatchet. That looks nothing like a 7.

I felt a little better just having it nearby, a testimonial to my twentieth birthday, to the morning in my apartment. In the back of my head, I could feel the 50, like a just-emptied rocking chair, always moving, always one part of my peripheral brain occupied. His birthday was in a month.

Lisa was sitting at the table, sorting through buttons.

The rest of the kids were in their chairs too, eyes awake, the spastic sleepy push of Monday in their blood. They seemed more or less healthy after their Friday bout with disease. I could hear the science teacher next door, voice bright and awake, unfired.

If the school had been a restaurant, I would've quit by now. Hung up my apron and washed my hands and walked off. More time to worry, to find a new job, the whole day free to torture or injure myself.

But instead, I stood myself up, tired and heavy, shoved the 50 out of my mind for the moment, and drew a big < on the board.

Good morning second grade, I said. Let's do something different today.

Bird beak! called out Lisa.

It's like a mouth, I said. Here we go. $1 < 2$. What do you think
that means?

The mouth is talking to 2 because it's mad at 1, said Lisa.

The mouth is talking to 2 because 1 is so boring, said Ann.

The mouth kisses 2 because 1 ignores him, said Elmer.

1 is number one, muttered Danny, miffed.

I smiled. I'd missed them. I'd almost been absent today.

Well, I said, breathing out, no. The mouth is always hungry,
and 2 is more than 1. The mouth always wants to eat the greater
one.

That's it? asked Lisa.

I wrote another: $55 > 23$.

John raised his hand. The mouth eats 55 because it's more, he
said.

Right, I said.

I erased the board.

You missed part of the 5, said Ann, pointing. There was just a
little chalk line left. I wiped it off. Ann couldn't concentrate unless
the board was cleared of fragments.

Next door, one of the third-graders in science class let out a
long moan.

These are called Greater Than and Less Than, I said, louder. I
put up 44 and 90. Brought Ellen to the front. I put up 2800 and
2300. Danny did that one. $>$, he wrote, in a dark slash. Mimi
goofed on 11 and 111, but as I was explaining the difference, someone next door let out a cough so rip-roaringly loud I thought he'd

expelled a lung. There was a smattering of applause from the science classroom.

Then I did something I probably shouldn't have done. I wrote on the board: Fake Sick   Real Sick.

I gave that to Ann, who walked up and did a bored < between the two. But the minute I'd written it up there, Lisa's energy had tripled, and she started hopping up and down in her chair.

I want to make one up! she said as soon as Ann was done. Can we make up our own?

I looked at the clock. We still had eleven minutes. The room had several chalkboards so I said okay, and told each kid to go ahead and stake out a space and write some numbers on the boards and we would all decide which was Greater, which was Lesser. Lisa pushed out her chair in a flash and the class followed suit. John wrote 5 and 1,000,000, and Mimi wrote 2 and 4, and Elmer was just starting to write when Lisa scrawled, in her big fast lopsided writing: Sick and Car Crash. Which is Greater Than? she announced to the class.

Everyone looked over.

Real Sick or Fake Sick? asked someone.

Real, said Lisa.

I'm tired of Lisa, said Ann, stuck with nothing on her board. Can we have free time?

I walked to Lisa's board, and picked up the eraser. That's different, I said. You can't compare these two. Try something else.

Outside, a girl slumped down the hall, crying for lemons.

I get scurvy this week, I heard Ellen whisper to Elmer.

Why not? Lisa said. She wrote a huge > on the board. Can-cer, she said. Woo-woo. She held her arms high in the air like the winner of a boxing match.

This upset Danny, who marched over to her board and swiped a chalk from the metal ledge and put War next to Sick. He made a mouth facing War so now it went War > Sick > Car Crash.

War beats cancer's butt, he said.

Lisa tried to grab the eraser from me. No way, she said.

I could feel the flutterings of helplessness in my chest.

Kids, I said.

Mimi piped in. I don't think car-crash people would like what you wrote, she said primly.

Cancer doesn't have a butt, said Ann.

Butt cancer does, said Danny.

I was in a car crash once, said Ellen.

John looked at her. No one else paid any attention.

By now Ann had walked to Lisa's board and written Old Age below the others. Put a > facing it.

Bo-ring, sang out Lisa. Pressing hard with the chalk, she wrote some huge thick letters to the left of War. And put a gigantic > by them. Now it said BLOODY MURDER > War > Sick > Car Crash. Old Age hovered quietly below.

Bloody Murder wins first place! said Lisa.

Now Ann tried to seize the eraser and so did Danny. Across the room, Elmer was fidgeting and squirming at the mention of bloody murder.

Sit down! I said, holding the eraser over my head. No one sat. I wrote Second Grade next to First Grade and made a > between the two. Elmer smiled again.

Sit down! I said. No one sat.

How do you spell *hand-to-hand combat*, asked Danny, urgent. Can I have the chalk?

We're about to finish up, I said. Sit.

Danny pointed to the flag in the corner of the room. His hand spluttered in the air. You wouldn't even be here, he said to Lisa.

Who's doing Numbers and Materials Friday? I asked.

I win! Lisa said.

Danny and Ann both glared at her.

You win nothing, said Danny.

The rest of the class slipped notebooks and papers into their brightly colored backpacks. The clock clicked back.

Me, said Mimi. I'm making something.

The class waited, poised, tight and hunched, until the bell rang, and then half ran out. Lisa walked straight to Danny and Ann and pushed them both with the spring of her fingertips, then Danny shoved her shoulder, and Elmer squealed, Fight! and for a second the air congealed into circus-alarm air. Lisa was closing her hand around Ann's ponytail but I walked over as Ann's face was imploding and Danny's knuckles were folding and grabbed Lisa away and held her back but I didn't quite do it right. She was out from under me in a second.

Bench time all week for the three of you! I said, catching Lisa's wrist. She struggled against me. No! she said. Right before Danny left the room, he went over to the flag and said something quiet to it, as if he were in church.

All week! I said, writing on the board. All of you!

Lisa broke out of my hand and ran straight to Ann's chalkboard where she wrote Lisa and Ann and then put a $>$ between the two. Ha! she yelled, dashing through the door.

Ann erased the board in two swipes and looked at me square-on before she left. You should have better class control Ms. Gray, she said. Her eyes were cold.

When she was gone, I sat on the table and looked around. On Elmer's board was Good Me > Bad Me.

I started shaking. And laughing a little. My hands were shuddering and a few tears shook out. I was wiping my eye when there was a tap at the door and in walked my boss. I went straight to Lisa's board and began erasing, fast.

Good morning Mona, she said, eyeing the remains of BLOODY MUR as they swept off the chalkboard.

She took a look around the classroom, taking in the spilled box of crayons, the leaking button drawer. She didn't seem to notice the ax.

The students seem to be enjoying your class, she said.

I waited for her to fire me for firing the science teacher on Friday.

What is it you were teaching today? she asked.

Oh nothing, I said, blowing dust off the eraser. I wiped off War > Sick. Just today I was teaching Greater Than and Less Than, I said.

The boss sat in one of the kid chairs, where she looked odd in her beige suit, the perfect clothing item for a Monday.

I'd like to ask a favor of you, Mona, my boss said.

I waited, at the chalkboard, dust swirling. I would not apologize for firing the science teacher. That is impossible, I would say. I practiced in my head.

I want you to keep an eye on Lisa Venus, she said. Her mother is worried about her but can't be around as much as she'd like and you seem to be Lisa's favorite teacher (I blushed at this even though I knew it was true) and we're concerned. Last week, she apparently brought cigarettes in her lunch.

Oh, I said, perking up a bit. But not to smoke.

You knew about this? my boss asked.

It was her theme lunch of the day, I said. Bologna and margarine and a saccharin drink and cigarettes.

My boss smiled, thinly. Mmmm, she said. Cute.

Do you get the theme? I asked.

Mona, she continued, you should *always* alert me when you see a child bringing cigarettes to school.

I'll keep an eye on her, I said.

Good, she said, seeming relieved. Good. Good. And Mona? she said.

She walked to the door and shut it.

Lisa's a very troubled little girl, she said. We're quite concerned about her.

I nodded about five times. The clock clicked back again, paused, clicked forward. I said: We?

People at the hospital, she said. Doctors. Her mother. They say she's behaving oddly.

She reached over to the table, and began putting the loose crayons back in their slots. She was careful to arrange them in color order. Blues next to greens, reds next to oranges. This irritated me.

Her voice dropped a decibel. You're of course aware of the situation with her mother.

I nodded. I am of course aware, I said.

She looked vaguely disappointed that I already knew.

They think sometime this spring, she said.

I felt like ripping her hair out in fistfuls now.

Now is it my imagination, she said, or did it say Bloody Murder on the chalkboard?

I pretended to dust chalk off my clothes. Never mind, she said. Glad we've had our discussion. You have a good afternoon now Mona. I'll see you later for Back-to-School Night.

Back-to-School Night? I asked.

She pursed her lips.

Tonight, she said. I put a note in your cubby. I've put several notes in your cubby in fact, she said.

I have a cubby? I asked.

Her voice was clipped. Seven P.M., she said. See you then.

12

That evening, before Back-to-School Night, I walked the three blocks to my parents' house to see if my father was worse. My mom's car wasn't in the driveway, which meant she was working late, making brochures, but I went in anyway. The house was dark, TV off, and no one seemed to be home, but then movement caught my eye and I looked through the living room window which was clear in the darkness and through it I saw my father planted in the backyard, standing alone on the grass, his face concentrated and serious, left leg extended behind him in a hurdle stretch.

Hi, I yelled through the glass. What's going on?

He jumped when he heard my voice, startled, but didn't turn around to face me. He was doing some trick with his arms, pushing outward from his chest, then reaching down to touch his foot.

I went outside.

It smelled more like fall than it does in fall, and I couldn't figure out why, and then I saw that he'd burned a circle into the grass, like a brand, a circle with a break in it, a shape something like this:

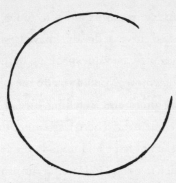

And he was standing smack in the middle.

Hello, I said, louder, worried, wondering what was happening. What's going on? It's Mona.

He turned around a bit then. He looked deeply embarrassed.

I'm just stopping by before Back-to-School Night, I said. Are you feeling okay?

He stayed in the circle. I'm just trying something out here, he said. I read about it in a book; it's written by a Harvard medical professor. I know it looks ridiculous. It's called *The Shape of Health*, he said, indicating the burnt grass around him. It's a reliable book. It's for athletes, he said.

I walked closer.

Don't come in, he said, voice urgent. There's only room for one.

I stopped right where I was. He carefully replaced his left leg with his right. See, they say the disease goes out that way, he said, pointing to the gap. You've got to push it outward. Push it off. It seems worth a try. There have been studies. According to the book, Olympic athletes who are ill use it. For some reason it has helped a fair number of people. He exhaled, breath slightly ragged, and pulled in his right leg, reaching down to touch both his feet. His back made a crooked curve in the air. I have to stay in the circle for just a few more minutes, he said, speaking to the ground. Did you say you're going downtown? Could you do me a favor? he asked.

I was standing there and watching him. I felt clearly that I should not have come over. There was something so terrible and private about this act of hope and it made me feel sickened to see him out there, stuck inside a circle doing running stretches, alone, before his wife came home from her job greeting tourists, when she herself had not left town in ten years.

He didn't look over. I can go by downtown, sure, I said. I leaned my hand out to a potted plant and knocked the thin spindled branches.

Could you pick up some more of that plant food at Jones's store? Your mother isn't going to be too happy about the state of the grass here. That other package was terrific but I already ran out.

Sure, I said, knocking. I'll go do that right now, I said. Sorry to interrupt. Are you doing okay? My voice was a notch higher than usual.

He leaned his head toward me but kept his eyes outward, looking out the opening of the hole.

Thanks honey, he said. I'm just trying to keep an open mind here, he said.

I turned around, ready to leave him in there and get out the front door because I thought I might suddenly shake into tears, when he let out a deep breath, stood straight, stepped free of the circle, and walked over to me, face ashy. I backed into the living room.

Look at that pretty dress, he said to me. How's teaching?

Do you want the same grass food as before? I asked. Are you worse?

He sat down on the living room couch and pulled a tissue from a box, using it to wipe his brow. I didn't want to look at him so I stared at the backyard, empty now, wondering where the illness was supposed to go once it left the circle. I pictured the entire backyard teeming with locusts. Crusting leaves and holed petals. A swish of darkness. But everything outside looked green as ever. Everything inside remained tepid and beige.

It's for athletes, he had said.

My father shifted on the couch. Any kind is good, he said.

He didn't answer my second question.

I heard my mom's car pull into the driveway and I told him, talking too fast, that I'd drop by with it as soon as I could. He was gone again, distracted, and sat on the couch, leaning forward to turn on the TV. I said good-bye and he said have fun, and both of us seemed embarrassed and uncomfortable, and I mumbled something about Harvard being a school of good studies and he nodded into the TV. His face was sallow as usual but the hope hanging around it made him look worse than ever. I went outside and waved at my mother, who was settling her things together in the car, and she waved back and smiled out the car window at me. She liked seeing me in a dress. I wanted to go tell her everything in the safe small space of the car but also I knew my father had done it while she wasn't home and finished before she returned and that this was not something that I should share.

I checked my watch. I had just enough time. I walked fast, touching the rough bark of trees. As I passed lawn after lawn, I thought about my mother—closing the car door, entering the house, going to hug her husband whose brow is murky with sweat and he is saying: Honey, I'm going to lick this thing I tell you, I'm going to lick it, and she nods, nodding, because it gives her something to do with her head. She wears nightgowns to bed now and dreams about airplanes. He dreams of racing along the desert, all knees and blur, sand kicking up, the wind making his eyes tear, and he wakes with a start, three A.M., his heart beating fast, and thinks: Is it death? Is it life? And she wakes up too, a light sleeper, and her fingertips are cool as they check the beat inside his neck. It's dark and quiet, two people in the house, lying flat, only two left now, two until one, and they both fall asleep again with their fingers clustered together on his throat like plain pink jewelry. By morning, he has forgotten. She remembers, alone in the morning bed, eyes blinking at the wall, but he's out and about pouring cereal. The circle is dewy and the yard is the same. He is the same. She is the same. I walked and thought about that hole marking up the backyard, thought of going inside my own apartment, kneeling on the living room floor and carefully drawing a big circle in the carpet with the point of a high heel:

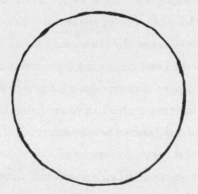

There. I'd go over the curves again and again until the carpet stems were beaten down and the circle was clearly defined. Then I'd tuck up my knees and curl up within it. Push it outward. Push it off. The

same as my father, except my circle would be complete, arc finished, with no break in it at all.

I'd had no intention of going downtown but I barreled straight
into the hardware store and found the same green plant food on
Aisle Four. Jones was, once again, absorbed in the newspaper on
his stool by the cash register. There were stacks of new tools on the
floor—bright wrenches just out of the box, piles of big blue buckets
against the wall with warnings about children drowning written on
the outside. How awful to die in a bucket, what an embarrassingly
small way to leave.

I took the plant food up to the counter.

Good thing I'm open late, was all he said.

Good thing, I echoed. I looked down, then back up, but he had
resumed reading by then, pages rustling. His fingers moved ex-
pertly into the bins of the cash register, handing over my change.
The newspaper was covering my view of the lump under his shirt,
and so I couldn't even guess if it was a bad day or a good one, neither revealed by the neutral expression across his face. I needed to
see the number, right then, to adjust mine according to his; if I
ever wanted desperately for him to recognize me and notice something, it was now, but he didn't even look up.

I crossed the street and walked through the park. When I
reached my mother's tourist office, and turned to look back, the
lights in the hardware store had gone out, and the sign on the door
was moving slightly, and read CLOSED in big simple black letters.

13

Back-to-School Night was swarming with people by the time I arrived, lights buzzing bright and yellow. I put the plant food in my classroom and stood by the table of cookies with rainbow speckles. Within seconds, Mimi's mother with the smooth blond hair came up to me. I wasn't sure she even knew who I was when she shifted the toddler in her arms, leaned in, and said: It's so fabulous how Mimi sees numbers in everything now! She calls her green beans ones, and makes her noodles into eights. Mrs. Lunelle beamed. Do you know where that new science teacher is? The toddler was squirming but she just held on tighter. I shook my head. Bye now Mona, Mrs. Lunelle said. Keep up the good work.

I was twitching slightly. My father is sick, I muttered, but she'd left.

As I stood there, eating a dry cookie with a chocolate blob in the middle, more parents came over to comment, to my surprise, on Numbers and Materials. I hadn't implemented it as a learning tool with any other class, and during schooltime the remaining groups did look on with envy as my second-graders marched into the classroom carrying lucky 7's cut from broken mirrors and small sailboat 4's. The reading teacher, a bland type, had tried to make a copied version of her own called Letters and Materials, but hers failed miserably after round one, A of applesauce.

She was here too, in her classroom, going over the sounds of the letters, *b-b-b*, so that parents could teach reading at home.

I filled a cup with tropical juice and took a post in my math room next to the gallery of numbers.

After a few minutes, Elmer Gravlaki's father dipped his head inside. He was a muscular man, with a lustrous auburn mustache and hands as solid as wheels, an absurd contrast to his spongy son.

He sat on the edge of the fleshy-colored table, which creaked under his weight. I am concerned about the Materials and Numbers, he said in his thick accent.

I raised my eyebrows in surprise. Elmer's math skills had been improving rapidly since we'd started.

He leaned in. I do not see, he said, how it is good for my business to have the children making addresses in your class.

Oh, they're not addresses, I said.

He finished his juice in a gulp, swiped red beads from his mustache.

No one's going to put an I.V. on a house, I said. No one is going to stick an 8 made of cough drops on their door.

He lifted his mustache to his nose and lowered it.

I have been making addresses in my workshop for twenty years now, he mumbled. He stood. I know where you live, he said.

The numbers on the wall fluttered from the wind of his exit. Sadly for both of us, this *I know where you live* thing was no threat to me—if he came to my apartment, fine. Maybe I could get him to chop off my foot. But there were two addresses for me, and the other was my parents' house. What if he got it wrong, poor Gustav Gravlaki, sneaking up to the window of their kitchen, storming into the living room. Oops. The house would wilt him in minutes. He'd turn into Elmer, instead of the other way around.

I left the room. Kids were everywhere, looking short and meek without day nearby to light them. I saw Ann holding her little sister's arm by the elbow. Lisa was getting herself a big plate of food; I waved and she shoved a red cookie in her mouth and waved back. Danny's one-armed father, George O'Mazzi the war veteran, was in the art room, right sleeve hanging loose as a shed snakeskin, deep in conversation with the art teacher, who was doing a melted-crayon demonstration. I didn't see the science teacher anywhere.

I found my cubby, stuffed to the brim. Mr. Gravlaki had his eyes on me, and was almost done with his paper plate of pepper crackers and celery boats when I noticed the door to the playground was ajar.

I walked over, brisk, slipped through.

Outside, it was much quieter, darker, the yellow of inside turned into the soft black of outside, the silhouettes of tree trunks and the metal climbing structure, and there was only one person out there, many feet away, turned to the side, moving his arms, a tall thin shadow.

And for a second I thought it was my father again. Still trying, still standing with his left leg behind him, still preparing to go running. And I wanted to head back in and close my eyes and get home and away instead of watching again and again as he tried, every backyard tested, the smell of burning grass on each block, the strangeness and largeness of his effort causing me physical pain, but then the man lowered his arm and the moment cleared and he became himself. A different man, younger, standing close to a mess of odd equipment.

And in another second, I recognized his shape.

The science teacher had a bubble wand made of string in his right hand, and a cigarette in his left. Leaning down, he dipped the wand into a bucket of soapy water, lifted it up, and pulled back on the string to form the bubble. It bloomed out, rainbowed and loose, jiggly, a belly of a bubble, and then while it wobbled in the air he brought up his left hand, sucked in on the cigarette, and, putting his mouth right to the open gap in the wand, released a puff of smoke inside. The smoke formed into a pearl within the curving pink and blue walls.

I tried not to move. The smoke and soap trembled together.

Attempting to keep it all balanced, he moved to seal the soap bubble around the smoke, but just at the last second his wrist twisted and the whole thing popped. The soap vanished and the pearl unraveled.

Fuck, he muttered. I smiled.

The air smelled like soap and ash; the liquid soap was the same brand I had once eaten in bar form, and so the clean smell reminded me of sex and vomit, but the dark smell of burnt paper and tobacco lit me up inside like gold; it was that familiar combination, illness and desire. I felt right at home.

I took a step forward.

He lost the wand in the bucket, fished it out, began another. The soap formed a glaze and then popped. He tried again. Pop. He tried again. A bubble cautiously emerged from the string, quivering on the wand. This one was big, a huge overweight bubble, leaning toward the ground. Raising up on his toes, he turned a bit as he lifted the wand, trying to give the bubble a chance, trying to raise it higher, and when he did that, he saw me.

Oh, he said. The bubble bent toward the asphalt and popped. I didn't know you were out here, he said.

There was a small amount of light from the school on him. He was wearing a T-shirt that said GO AWAY, and he looked different than usual. I'd never seen him at night before: eyebrows keened in, mouth slow and real, large hands.

I'd avoided him entirely since the scurvy day.

Do you want me to go? I asked.

No, he said.

They're very beautiful, I said.

He peered at me and nodded. Re-dipping the string, he started another bubble, but the wand slipped from his fingers into the bucket again.

I'm hiding out, he said. If anyone asks, this is a science demonstration. Spheres. Though they'll fire me if they see me smoking.

I didn't say anything to that, but a bundle of laughter loosened in my stomach, twine releasing, logs falling into the fire. He looked up.

I'm going for a record, he said, nodding. I want to see how many times I can get fired in one school year.

He shook soap off the wand.

I think you've won already, I said.

Just wait, he said. You're on my heels, he said. I saw that 5 made of meat the other day, that was the strangest thing I've ever seen.

Holding the cigarette like a dart, he brought it back to his lips and took in the smoke.

Last week, John had unpacked his lunch, peeled up the bread, and revealed a slab of steak from his mother's butcher shop cut in the shape of a 5, slathered with ketchup. I'd laughed for about ten minutes, watching him eat his sandwich, saying $5 - 2 = 3$ with his mouth full until he finished, swallowed, mumbled: $5 - 5 = 0$. I gave him extra credit when he wiped his mouth and said: That was a prime cut of meat.

Elmer's dad thinks I want to take over his address business, I said.

Mr. Smith laughed the smoke into the bubble. See? he said. You'll be fired in no time. We can start our own school, all math and science. Now that'll be a hit.

I put one shoe on my other shoe. He lifted the wand, very gently, up. The bubble slithered out.

About the other day, I said.

He shook his head. Go, he said to the bubble. You had your opinion, he said to me.

I pressed my heel down into my toe.

Lisa was doing cancer, I said.

Yeah, he said. I know. That girl just loves to do her cancer. These are actually her cigarettes, he said.

The heel dug deeper into the toe. I could feel my heart moving around in my ribs.

I think it's an awful assignment, I said.

He tried to finish and close off the smoke-filled bubble, but right before it completed, it popped. Poof.

Shit! he said. He put down the wand for a second and looked at me, rolling his mind back to the last thing I said.

That's okay if you do, he said. I don't.

Then he turned his attention back to the bucket. Stirred the soap mixture with his hand. I'm just learning how to do this, he said.

I imagined draping a slow-moving rainbow of bubble around his body, and watching it surround him, an aquarium. I was thinking about him liking his assignment. Trying to understand how anyone could possibly like that assignment.

You know her mom has some kind of new cancer, right? I asked.

He flicked a few ashes. Sure, he said. That's why she picks it.

And her mother is dying, you know that too, right?

He looked at me flat in the eye. Sure, he said. That's why she picks it.

He didn't move his eyes, and shook the string in his hand. I put my foot down and started to turn toward the door.

Leaving? he asked.

I didn't answer.

I wish you could see a whole one, he said. They're amazing. But the wand is broken or something, he said.

I was about to walk to the door but I hadn't moved yet. Stayed put. Nodded. I stared at him. He exhaled loudly. I nodded a second time. I nodded a third time. But I knew I could do it; that wand was not broken. I put my shoe back on my shoe, wobbling in the shadows, while burst ghosts of bubble shimmied into the air.

Can I try? I asked.

He blinked, cigarette/dart burning a small red circle in the air, poised to be thrown.

It's hard, he said.

Just to try, I said.

He shrugged and held forward the wand and the cigarette, which burned low, almost down to its filter.

I have to go back in ten minutes, I said, breathing in the soap smell of the bucket.

You can make one in ten minutes, he said, maybe.

I have ten minutes, I said again.

I took the wand awkwardly—it was sticky and slick—and dipped it into the soap bucket. I picked the cigarette from his fingers and let it stick out from my knuckles.

He stood back by the climbing structure, and let me be. He didn't do that thing that some men do, holding my elbow and guiding me through the motions, and I was so grateful that he wasn't touching me that I wanted, suddenly, acutely, for him to touch me.

I lifted the wand from the soap bucket and let the excess drip off. Someone inside the school broke something made of glass and there was a burst of laughter and a few murmurs of concern.

I held up the wand, windowed by soap. I pulled back on the string and the bubble began to poke out its face, slippery and glimmering.

My hand slacked on the wand and the bubble started to recede.

Careful, he said, four feet away, rising up on the balls of his feet. Keep a tight hold.

I did. The bubble stayed put. The smell swept over me. Inside, I heard apologies being made about the broken glass, and I heard the art teacher's high voice brushing them off—It's okay, it's okay.

I tensed my wrist, and taking the cigarette up to my lips with my other hand, sucked in. The smoke waited, patient, in my mouth, and I raised the swirling bubble with my arm, and released the smoke in a stream into the hole of the wand. It whooshed out of me: white, intimate.

I got ready to seal up the bubble and he was watching, I could feel him waiting, and I felt the bubble wobbling, and smelled the bucket and breathed in the smoke and I knew right then that mine would work. Mine would seal up, take off, and rise over our heads. A beautiful shuddering pearl in a sphere.

I felt him waiting for me, and I wrecked it.

The bubble popped obediently and the smoke spread and thinned in the air.

Oh, I said. Oh well.

He was watching me closely. You had it, he said.

Oh well, I said. I gave the nearby tree trunk a quick knock. My stomach unsettled. It's hard to do, I said.

He remained right where he was, by the side of the climbing structure.

You broke it on purpose, he said.

I didn't look over. Was that more than ten minutes? I asked, remembering. Time for me to go. The wand was limp in my hand and I balanced it on the edge of the bucket.

Do it again, he said. Make a quick one.

No, I said. I have to go now.

Hang on, he said. Tell me. Did you? Did you break it on purpose?

I could feel the night air underneath my dress. I kept the smell of the soap close; I was afraid of him moving forward, of the smoke caving around us, of his man hands.

He watched me closely. He had lit a new cigarette and was holding it in that same dart way, which looked even stranger now that it was full-length.

Well, he said, if you can do it, show me how.

The wand slipped down into the bucket. There was a faint ringing in my ears. I knocked on a tree trunk; the wood was bumpy.

I feel sick, I blurted. It's the soap. I have to go, I said.

He muttered something underneath his breath.

What? I said, holding out the cigarette to him, almost all filter now. Did you say die?

He shook his head. He reached over and took the cigarette back, touching my fingers for a second, and stubbed it out.

I started backing away. My stomach hurt. Thank you, I said. I've got to go but thanks, that was great. Sorry about the other day. I hope Mrs. Lunelle doesn't find you.

He kept looking at me. He fished the wand from the bucket; it slipped in; he swore, retrieved it, and started to make a half bubble—letting it poke out, pulling it back to flat.

Feel better, he said. See you tomorrow.

Thanks, I said, okay. You too.

I stopped at the door. I could see the art teacher now through a window, rings alive on her fingers, a few shards of glass at her feet.

He cleared his throat and was about to ask another question.

But I was now through the door and inside. I was in the bright room of plastic cups and needy parents. He was outside, air dark and clarified, attempting thin brief planets. When I looked back, I could barely see him whispering smoke into the new bubble.

He was facing the other way now and his T-shirt read COME BACK.

I got the plant food, said good-bye to my boss and a few key parents, and a special good-bye to Lisa, who was tagging along with Elmer's family for the night. I let her slap her fist into my open palm for a minute, but my stomach was hurting and I had to go. On the walk home, I knocked on every single tree I passed. On occasion I knocked twice, and so the walk home took twice as long. My stomach was upset and my hands were trembling. I knocked on one tree so hard I ruptured the skin on my knuckle. If I'd stayed, I thought, if I'd made more, what would've happened come end-of-evening? What. That lingering by the car door, or the school door, or worst: my front door. That door lingering, I couldn't do it. I would not touch a man who disagreed, who knew when I folded; I would have to swallow the bucket to combat that. I would have to drink an entire bubble bath. I would drown in that blue bucket of lather and froth.

That night I lay close to the potted plant, knocking up a storm. I'd finish knocking and then I wouldn't *feel* finished and I'd have to knock again. I wondered what glass it was that had broken in the art teacher's classroom. A water glass? A window. A pair of glasses? A knickknack from Finland. A glass eye? A slipper. My fingers. My skin.

My glass watch face: break it. Fist down, smash the glass. The two hands halt. The longest ten minutes of my life. Is the ten minutes up yet? I look down. Nope, I say, even though the sun is rising now. Ten minutes aren't up yet. I have to go in ten minutes but I still have ten minutes left. Let me make another bubble. Let me show you how it's done. Three years later, all the soap is used and the kids are grown and the air is clear and the bucket is dry. Me and the man are sprawled out on the asphalt—lungs deteriorated, fingers pruned, legs interlaced. Clean and tired.

I'm hungry, I tell him, squeezing his hand. He nods, and we slip through the gate into the day.

14

The same week of high school that I quit track, I missed a math test. I never missed math tests but woke up that morning and something about the sun through the curtains, rolling out its smooth ivory rays, made me unable to move. The world can ask you to participate, but it's a day-by-day decision if you want to agree to that proposal. When I didn't show up in the rest of the house, my mother wandered into my room, put a cool palm on my forehead, declared me tepid, but said I could stay home if I wanted.

I spent most of the day in bed. I got up once and sat outside, looking over at Mr. Jones's backyard of dark bushes, thinking of him in front of the class, trying to convey the sweet enigma of x, nobody paying attention with me not there.

I wanted to stay home all week. I wanted to stay in bed for the rest of my life, until the mattress fell apart and threw me to the floor. I was afraid of going to school, turning a corner, and finding the track coach in her navy blue sweatpants and slight earnest accent, recruiting coltish freshmen. The thought of it made me want to throw up. I tried to stay in bed again the following morning, but this time my mother swatted me out the door. My father drove to work, wearing a suit the color of dirty water.

I walked the high school halls close to the wall, thinning myself, skittish, buglike, and so, when in math class that afternoon Mr. Jones told me I had to stay after to take the makeup test, I was flooded with relief. Anything to keep me out of the school at large. It's all word problems, he said. I felt the calmest I'd felt all day in the math classroom, which had both its doors wide open to the afternoon sun. After the bell rang, I stayed in my seat and the rest of the students ran out. Mr. Jones blew his nose and came over to my desk.

The lump under his shirt was medium-sized, and from what I could tell it was fat enough to be double digits but not fat enough to be in the twenties. I guessed his old favorite.

15? I said, pointing.

He smiled a little, face soft and tired. And nodded. Very good, he said. Very good.

He had the paper in his hand.

Nobody likes makeup tests, and I was still nursing a stomach-ache from walking through the hallways, but the truth is I ended up being very grateful for that day. Not because of the shelter it provided, even though I was glad for that, and not because I needed to learn more about algebra, a subject I knew well already, but because it was during that makeup test that the first and only person ever noticed and commented on my knocking. Until that moment, I'd been living in my own little universe of good-luck hell. I was subtle about knocking, usually doing it before falling asleep, like prayer time, but I was still surprised that the people I knew well weren't more aware. My parents didn't notice, my lunchtime friends didn't notice, and later on, even that one boyfriend didn't notice (although he did say once, in the middle of sex, Mona, MONA, *what* are you doing with the bedframe?). It was only Mr. Jones, the hypocrite of my childhood, who observed and remarked on my engine of a hand.

He handed over the paper and a pencil.

Go to it, he said. You have twenty-five minutes. I'll be right up here if you have any questions.

I nestled into my chair. In general, I find math tests soothing; all those numbers on the page nervous and undone, waiting for me to come over and settle them into their right spots.

But the first word problem made me uncomfortable immediately and it just got worse from there.

Janet can run 50 yards in 30 seconds on Tuesday. She runs 15 percent faster on Wednesday, but on Thursday she runs 5 percent slower than that. How fast does she run on Thursday?

I skipped Question One, which made my hand pull into a fist, knocking briefly on the test paper.

Question Two was worse.

Janet is the fastest runner on the team until Lydia moves in from Kentucky. Lydia runs twice as fast as Janet on Monday, but then four times slower on Tuesday. How fast does Janet run on Tuesday?

I knocked again. Mr. Jones looked up.

Is someone at the door? he asked. His eyes looked tired, bagged, underlined with arcs from endless correcting. I could see the 15 sinking. His change when he drove home, the quick swap for 12, for 7, for 4.

Oh no no, I said. I think they just left.

Eyes on your own paper, he said, out of habit. I smiled. The classroom was empty aside from the two of us.

Outside, lockers were being opened and slammed and students were talking loud, glowing with three o'clock, everyone hungry for everything.

I read Question Three: Janet wins another race. Question Four: Janet in training. Question Five: Janet goes to the Olympics.

I could feel the ache growing in my stomach, and put my fist down to the paper and knocked again. Dragged my knuckles over the white space. Slow Janet down. The only class I've ever failed was driver's training, because I spent the whole time touring the town with my foot slammed against the brake.

Question Six: Janet in the prelims at the Olympics held in Slovenia. Question Seven: Janet as the anchor in a four-way race with two variables.

Knock knock knock. I rubbed my knuckles against the words. I tried to concentrate just on the numbers. But there was even a drawing at the bottom of the page of a girl with muscular thighs running, lines whisking off her back to indicate the immensity of her speed. Hurrying to another page, that busy beaming Janet.

I knocked again and this time he caught me.

Mona Gray? he said. He stood up.

I think it's some pipes banging, I said, indicating outside.

Oh no, he said. I saw you just then. I saw that.

I'm almost done, I said.

Question Eight: Janet racing a train and winning.

I pretended to look at the page and concentrate but I had to knock again. I tried to imagine her dead on the ground: a snail, a robot, a corpse in running shorts. I glued Janet to the bleachers and chained her with a metal ring to the bench leg. I deliberately broke my pencil lead.

Oops, I said. Look at that.

Mr. Jones was standing right by me now, looking down with curiosity. He perched himself on the neighboring desk, the one where Greg Fitzpatrick usually sat and flung his eyes back like a fishing line to cheat.

Question Nine: Janet running in outer space, beating two comets and an asteroid.

Mona Gray, he said, what exactly are you doing with that paper there?

I faced him. I pulled in my lips.

What do you mean? I asked.

He indicated with his chin. I mean, he said, why do you insist on knocking on this piece of paper? He picked up the test and put it back down.

I don't know, I said. I'm knocking on wood, I said.

He blinked at me over the desk. He was wearing a shirt that said Minehead over the pocket. I wondered if that was his first name.

Knocking on wood, he echoed.

Yes, I said.

Why? he asked.

What?

Why are you knocking on wood?

I stared at him. The question itself bothered me enough that I had to knock, and I reached down to the paper again. We both watched my hand go. I felt like a zoo animal.

Well if you don't stop I'm going to have to deduct from your grade, he said. You're giving me a headache.

I'm sorry, Mr. Minehead, I said. I mean Mr. Jones.

He breathed in and shrugged. Knocking on wood, he murmured.

Question Ten: Janet on the high school track in a race against Death, Death wearing a black fashionable running outfit, quick and ruthless, sweaty and swift; Death loses by thirty seconds.

I finished reading and held up the paper. I'm done now, I said. I fluttered it in his face. I wanted to get the page away from me. I didn't even like having my hand close to those words.

He raised his eyebrows and plucked it like a kerchief from my fingers.

I looked away, out the two open doors of the classroom. I could still see people walking to the stairways, readying to leave school for the day and do teenager things, like sit in closets together, reaching out tentative hands until they crossed the air and hit skin. There were so many colors and sounds that happened when the classes dismissed. They overwhelmed me. The reds and the blues alone were so rich I could've stared at them for hours.

Mr. Jones was turning over my paper. There's nothing on here, he said.

I needed to knock again. But he had the paper now, and the desk, although grainy and brown, was definitely not wood. I zipped open my backpack and stuck my hand in there, near my notebook, near the stacks of paper, the dead leaflets from trees all stuffed inside to save me.

I couldn't do it, I said.

He peered at me over his glasses. You? he said. You couldn't do it? You?

I felt like I might start to cry.

No, I said, small.

Why not? he said. And my hand was rummaging around now in the backpack for a loose piece of paper, and finally I spotted my pencil in the elongated pencil dish on the desk and pulled out my hand and knocked that, the slim curved wood back, number two lead, gentle and subtle, so slight a knock he couldn't possibly notice.

But he did. He was Mr. Jones. He watched my hand knock the pencil.

Knocking on wood, he said, pointing.

My throat was closing, and my eyes were getting glassy. I finished up and moved my hand away.

That's right, I said. That's right.

He smiled a short smile, trying to be encouraging. I looked down at my hand, right hand, knocking hand, and for one shattering second felt known. I loved him right then, a love fiercer in balance against the hate I still felt since he'd never commented on my father. He was the only one who'd ever noticed the knocking. Or maybe more likely: the only one who was brave enough to ask.

Why didn't you do the test? he asked again.

I have a problem with running, I said.

He continued to stare at me for a minute. I blinked back the glass from my eyes as best as I could. Like riverbanks just under flood level, the water rose to the surface, voluptuous at the edge, and then, blessedly, receded.

I've seen you run, he said then. You're good.

I concentrated on clearing my eyes without using my hands. I had nothing to say to that.

Mr. Jones put the webbing between his thumb and forefinger at his lips and held it there for a minute. We were both quiet and four locker doors slammed outside. Some girl let out a big laugh, off the top of her head, that had no joy in it at all. The boy she was with made some more jokes.

Did you know, said Mr. Jones, speaking into his hand, that

some woman in Texas typed out all the numbers from one to a million? He rubbed the webbing over his lips.

That would fill a lot of paper, I said.

Took her a few years, he said. He pressed his cheeks down with his fingers. Knocking on wood, he repeated.

I listened politely. I had, at that point, been knocking since my dad got sick, so that was six years of knocking. Maybe a million knocks on a million papers by now.

Finally, Mr. Jones removed his hand from his mouth. I wondered if he was going to give me some advice but he just said, You may go now Mona Gray. We bent heads gently at each other. I stood, and exited his classroom. The afternoon was still light and bright, and I followed the footprints of the world of teenagers back to my parents' house, into the ashen living room, turned on the lead TV, slept a sleep about stones and storm clouds and rats and forks.

A few days later, Mr. Jones gave me a retake, where all the running words had been fully crossed out with black marker and replaced by swimming words. The girl at the bottom, Janet, now had a pool built around her fast muscled body, a cap over her hair, and a towel drawn by her feet. I did it in about ten minutes and got an A.

Two years later he quit the school and opened the hardware store. Opening day was a mob scene, flooded with townspeople, shoving each other aside to pick the choicest hammers and pliers off the walls. The school tried to woo him back, but Jones told everyone he was tired of correcting tests and explaining exponents and now wanted more than anything to sell every kind of nail. Tools, he announced, are the wave of the future. I hadn't seen him in a while, and wandered the aisles, anonymous; I did not say hello or reintroduce myself, but instead checked the size of the shape under his shirt: double digits, fat enough across to be in the 20's or even 30's. He seemed happy. I watched as the bins emptied of supplies. I didn't buy anything myself, and when the people started to clear out, bags full, brimming with the particular happiness that comes from purchasing tools, I left the store and walked home. Usually Jones's good moods uplifted me, but that afternoon I was subdued and slow, and our numbers were different.

15

I visited my father the morning after Back-to-School Night. I forgot to bring the plant food and said I would soon; he thanked me anyway, folding the wax paper that held the cereal into an envelope. I said, Do you feel all right? He said sure, didn't he look all right? He was awaiting the results from his *Shape of Health*. I put a hand on his forehead. He felt regular temperature. I asked him how his heart was. He lay his fingers on his beating neck and listened. I asked him if he felt weaker than usual. I could see his eyes fade off, measuring.

The thing about 51 is it's the first number in all the numbers that has nothing going on. It's not a prime, or a special semiperfect number, or a sum of any factors; 51 is the smallest digit with no magic inside of it. This in itself makes it interesting, but interesting in the way a cement block in the middle of a field of poppies is interesting. I have a book called *Your Favorite Numbers* and on 51 it just says: If this is your favorite number you are the type of person who is drawn to the most bland, banal dog at the pound simply because no one is paying any attention to it at all.

This was the number it looked like my father might not turn.

On the way out, I made my mother promise to call if anything ever happened. Mona, she said, worrying doesn't do anything.

So then don't worry about me worrying, I said back.

At school, I avoided the science teacher the best I could. I ate lunch in my classroom and exited school through the side door. On Friday, listening to the now-familiar sound of retching in his room, I taught more subtraction to the second grade using word problems about the kids in the class: Ann DiLanno grew five heads in September and by October had only two heads. How many heads did she lose?

I have one head, Ann interrupted. I am not losing a single head.

I was fidgety because it was Friday, which meant tomorrow was Saturday, and after Saturday was Sunday, and that was two days of no work and all worry.

In fact, no one seemed to be in a very good mood.

Every morning now, Danny walked in and thanked the flag; he made sure to do this when Lisa was in the room. Today, Lisa went to the bathroom and returned to the front of the class with the I.V. on her head again.

Oh look, said Ann, Intra.

Sitting with a finger up inside each curl, Mimi said: Lisa, it's me today for Numbers and Materials, you're not up again.

I know, said Lisa.

I dusted chalk off my shirt. Mimi kept her fingers inside her curls the way some kids eat olives. I told Lisa to sit down. She walked by, and let out a lung-splitting cough right in my face.

Spit sprinkled my cheeks and nose.

Cover your mouth, said Mimi, disgusted.

I thought you didn't get colds, I said, wiping my eyes.

Lisa fell to the floor and had a coughing fit, dark clouds caught in her ribs. I crouched down, about to hit her on the back, when Ann called from her chair: Ms. Gray, can't you tell by now? She's just doing science class again.

Lisa's cough stopped, cleanly. I held my hand in midair.

I never get colds, Lisa said, then sat back in her chair.

I felt like walking out.

The class blinked: fourteen eyes, fringed bees.

Thank you Ann, I said slowly.

I'm tired of all the other choices, Lisa said from her seat. Show me how to do your dad.

I cleared my own throat and turned away from her. Wrote 20 − 11 on the board.

So class, I said. What do you do if you have a zero in the ones place?

Lisa had a small epileptic seizure in her chair.

Like that? she asked.

John raised his hand. You borrow, he said.

That's right, I said. Borrow what? I kept my voice steady.

Lisa slumped on her desk and her eyes sagged and mouth drooped. Or this, she slurred.

Take the two to one, John said. I slashed the two on the board and wrote a small one above it. John nodded.

Lisa was now wheezing shallowly. Or maybe this, she panted. I could hardly stand to look at her.

When do I get to go for Numbers and Materials? asked Mimi.

I turned to Mimi brightly. How about right now, I said. Lisa lolled her head off her chair and groaned.

Since the parents' enthusiasm on Back-to-School Night, I'd made Numbers and Materials a bigger focus of the week. Even Ann seemed to be coming around, bringing in a 100 made from rhinestones, on a stickpin, which she'd said was a gift. Terrific! I'd said, pinning it to my blouse. I will live forever, I'd thought. But I have to get it back by the end of the day, Ann had said. It's a day-long gift. Sure enough, at the end of the day she'd approached me with palm out. I took it off, but I wasn't really bothered until I saw that she didn't put the stickpin away but instead brought it over to another teacher, the art teacher, who then put it on with equal happiness. I was annoyed simply because I am the math teacher and I didn't understand why it was appropriate for anyone but me to get a stickpin with 100 on it.

Once called on, Mimi went to her purple backpack and removed a plastic bag. Lisa raised her head to watch. But when Mimi opened the bag, before I saw a thing, I smelled it first, wham, transport, and the taste of acid sizzled in my throat.

Wait, Mimi, I said suddenly. On second thought, I said, let's do something else.

What? Mimi said.

I wondered if I might vomit all over the carpet.

Word problems, I said. Mimi, share that at lunch. Ann had seven heads—

Mimi's face froze. I want to share my Number and Material! she said. I've spent all week on it!

Bring out your workbooks, I said.

The whole class started talking all at once. You can't stop in the middle! they said. This is Numbers and Materials! This is NUMBERS and MATERIALS! Danny stood. I walked to the back of the room. Elmer dove under his chair. Lisa stared at me.

Mimi's eyelashes were birthing tears.

The smell in the room was so thick I had to plug my nose. Which helped a little.

It took hours and hours! said Mimi. Her voice snagged on the words.

I put my other hand on my stomach. Kept my nose closed. Danny had grabbed up a handful of rubber bands, and was finding the heaviest and thickest, the one that had once held broccoli together, and Lisa Lisa Lisa now had her own hand pinching her own nose, and when I saw that I wanted to burn down the school so I took another step back and nodded at Mimi. Said Go. Now.

Two tears dripped down her face.

Lisa kept staring at me. I didn't look at her, but took my hand off my nose and opened up the throat. Within seconds, Lisa had dropped her hand too. I felt an unexpected whale of loathing for her.

With utmost care, Mimi reached down into her backpack and brought out a huge 9 made of soap. I don't know where she possibly could've found such an enormous piece of soap, but the 9 was as tall as my forearm. Just the sight of it made my stomach seize.

Danny put down the rubber bands. Mimi brushed her cheeks dry.

I leaned on the far wall.

Do your thing from there Mimi, I said, keeping my nose passage plugged. I'm just going to stand here, I said, and see if you're talking loud enough.

So Mimi, still sniffing, shouted her whole presentation, telling us about how 9 was her favorite number because it was how old her older sister was and also her bedtime and she said it all so loud that most of the kids had to clamp their hands over their ears. She continued by doing some subtracting on the board, in her curly girly handwriting, and finished by telling everyone that before lunch they could wash their hands with her 9.

We will subtract from it more, she said.

She looked up at me, eyes clear. She'd prepared that sentence all week.

She passed around the 9 and the class was especially nice, pretending to shower with it, and before the bell rang I kept a hand near my mouth and assigned Danny next week's Numbers and Materials.

I could hear the class sigh with relief, that it wasn't all over.

Yes! Danny said. I know exactly what I'm going to bring. He gloated at Lisa.

When class was dismissed, I went straight to the medicine chest and took a stomach pill. Found an empty bathroom stall and knelt in front of the toilet. Held my arms around my waist. It was as if a ghost had entered the classroom, invisible but focused, arms warm, snaking around my waist, lips like wind on the neck. My body waking up, in math class, the wrong place to be woken up. And sickened. And awakened. And nauseous. And distracted.

I stayed in the bathroom for five minutes. My stomach heaved a couple times but nothing came out. When I could stand to go outside, I straightened my legs, and for just one second my fingers crept inside my shirt and rode the skin of my stomach up and found my breast and held it. So swift, soft, and there was my breast just sitting there, handless, waiting for me to do that. All my skin rose up to meet me.

I flushed the empty toilet and went outside for recess duty.

I looked for the science teacher, wondering what would happen if I saw him right then, right then, or right then.

On the yellow plastic bench, I breathed in the mild afternoon air. After a few minutes, Lisa, wearing her I.V. as a belt now, ran over and sat next to me. It's the last day of bench time, she said. Will you tell me when fifteen minutes is up? I checked my watch. Across the playground, Danny was sitting on the orange plastic bench, kicking his legs. Ann was on the blue plastic bench, arms folded. Lisa sat quietly next to me. I asked her if she remembered why she was benched and she said yes, she was benched because her mother had cancer.

No no, I said, that's not it at all, Lisa, it's because you shoved Danny and Ann on Monday, remember?

Oh yeah, she said vaguely.

John kicked a home run. I kept deep-breathing. Lisa asked if I was okay. She said I looked pale and flushed.

You were awful today, she said. You can't *ever* take away Numbers and Materials, she said.

She studied the kickball game for a while. Elmer missed the ball four times in a row.

I didn't much like your fake cough either, I said.

Lisa filled her cheeks with air, popped them, then turned her head and looked at me.

Sorry I spit on you, she said.

I looked back. Pieces of sleep were parked in the corners of her eyes, and her face seemed small and seven years old.

I won't take away Numbers and Materials, Lisa, I said.

She turned her eyes away, fast, and I saw them fill with water, brief and bright.

You know, she said after a bit, some people like to keep it secret
and maybe you shouldn't tell all the other kids, but I am different
and I would want to know.

Want to know what? I asked.

When you got cancer, she said.

My shoulders sank a whole level lower. I almost smothered
Lisa, I felt such a quick and crushing wave of love for her.

I just had a little stomach problem, I said, but I'm better now.
I don't have cancer, I said.

Stomach cancer, she said.

No, I said, smiling a little.

There's such a thing, she said.

I put my hand around her shoulder and squeezed her. She was
wearing a yellow T-shirt that used to say SUN on it but the letters
were falling off and now it just said N. I know, I said, but that's not
it; it's Mimi's 9. It's nothing to worry about, I said. I just can't handle the smell of soap.

Why not? she asked.

Allergic, I said.

No one's allergic to soap.

I am, I said.

She shook her head.

Lisa had been having a bad week, hair rattier than ever. I'd
brought a hairbrush on Tuesday and tried to use it on her during
lunch, but combing through those bundles was like walking
through peanut butter. The prongs kept sticking in her hair and
one broke off and got lost. She had no one to make lunch for her at
the hospital, and kept showing up at school with thematic lunches
she'd made herself, like the entirely orange lunch of carrots,

oranges, and cheddar cheese. Or the circular lunch of crackers, cucumber slices, and bologna. Or that Cancer Lunch, which consisted of some combination of salami or bologna with margarine on white bread, smoked fish, fake sugar packets, and cigarettes, wrapped in tin foil, all to be eaten in direct sunlight.

Or what she called the invisible lunch, which happened most often of all.

My parents used to wash out my mouth with soap, I told her. So the smell reminds me of that.

She took that in, heels kicking around.

Is your father contagious? Lisa asked.

Out on the playground, I saw the art teacher tell Danny his fifteen minutes were done, and he got up and began chasing Elmer around the kickball field, and Elmer's running was so slow even Danny got bored and ran off to torment someone faster.

Snail! he yelled as he left Elmer behind.

144 Main! Elmer cried back.

Ann slipped off her bench and went to the kickball field, never once unfolding her arms, a human envelope.

I wasn't sure what to do with Lisa's question. It kept slipping out of my mind. How's your mom doing? I asked instead. Lisa slid off the bench and walked away.

It's not time yet, I said, but I looked at my watch and she was right.

Mimi ran over with the huge slippery 9 in her hands, losing its clean numerical form, pawed by the dirty fingers of a million kids. She offered it forward.

I can't, I said. Sorry about earlier, Mimi. You worked really hard on this.

My stomach was acting up all over again, just looking at it.

She seemed hurt anyway. Ms. Gray, she said, subtract!

She brought it closer to my face and I felt like I might choke, or take off my clothes, or both at the same time, and I told her to stop, please, that I was allergic, to please take it away. Then she looked guilty. She ran back to the kickball field and they used it as a kickball for a while, and Lisa joined the game, which I was relieved to see.

When classes were done, and my school day was over, I did pass the science teacher in the front hallway, picking up his black coat. I thought of pushing him into the bushes, breaking his face open with mine. I could taste the soap skein hovering on the air. I considered leaving my stuff and going out the side door like usual, but he saw me first.

He didn't say anything. I waited for some kind of greeting.

I waited. I considered turning away before he greeted me. I stopped. I could turn away. He was looking right at me, but he wasn't saying anything.

I walked over.

Hello, I said then.

Hello, he said.

I put on my jacket. He had more stains and burns all over his arms.

So, I said, how are those scurvy kids doing?

He put his hands in his pockets. Good, he said. They just get sicker and sicker each week.

I picked up my bag and opened the door, and we walked through it, into fresh air, away from the sounds of a hundred kids hitting each other.

I'm going home, I said.

I'm going to the matinee, he said.

I nodded.

It's at four, he said. I passed a tree on the left and slapped the bark with my palm. The smell of three-o'clock sunshine felt like someone had broken open the sky.

I don't like movies, I said. I have two minutes, I said.

He smiled, but didn't look over. We kept walking. We rounded the corner.

I didn't mean you should come with me, he said after a bit. You don't have to lie about it.

In the distance the blue hospital rose up against the sky, a jelly-fish against water.

Excuse me? I said.

By the way, I can make the bubbles now, he said. I remembered how you did it and now I can do it.

He had his head tilted back, looking at the leaves above us while we walked. We went through the vacant lot, stepping on tall whitish weeds. A woman in a baseball cap was carefully polishing the iron geese on her lawn with a cloth.

I don't like to be accused of lying, I said.

He shoved his hands deeper in his pockets.

Well, he said.

What?

Well, except that was a lie too, he said.

I could still find the soap smell in my nose. A couple of people walked by: boy and girl. He had a hand hovering at her back, un-sure whether or not it was okay to touch. She was walking an inch ahead of his hand, pushed by the air between them.

I cleared my throat. So what movie? I asked.

The science teacher gave a matching cough up to the trees. Mona, he said, there's only one movie ever playing.

My face curdled with annoyance.

So, I said.

It's been two minutes, he said.

I have five minutes, I said.

We were almost at my apartment. If I followed the pattern, I'd go in and stare at the 50 for the rest of the day, but the idea of sitting on that sofa and having the same awful afternoon I always had made my throat close.

The apartment loomed, we walked up to it, I looked at the window that was mine. We walked past.

I should go to the hardware store, I said. I need some nails.

He rubbed his forehead. It's a cop movie, he said. You have more than five minutes?

I hate cop movies, I said.

He smiled again. I felt like destroying him. He didn't say anything more, and we kept walking, past the houses, fences, windows, cars, driveways, lawns, sprinklers, trees, sidewalks, front doors, address after address, each assigned and made individually by Elmer Cravlaki's father, some iron, some wood, some plastic, one made of glass that shone over the front door in a wind-chime bauble of numbers. We'd been quiet for long enough and I wasn't sure what to do in the space so I told him I was glad he could do the bubbles, and that I was worried about Lisa Venus. He said it was lucky Lisa had me.

I don't think she's doing too great, I said. Her hair's a wreck, she keeps doing your stupid fake disease stuff, she has no one making her lunch, and she asked me today, for the second time, if I was sick. I kicked a flat black rock on the sidewalk.

His voice was agreeable. So, he said, what did you say?

I cleared my throat. I had an urge to put the rock back. I said no, I said. What do you mean? What would you say?

He looked right at me. I'd say no, he said.

And there was something different in his tone then and it made me need to knock so I paused the way some people do to tie their shoe and went over to the tall skinny sidewalk tree with the peppery bark and hit it, knock knock knock knock, inhale, exhale. He waited for me. He didn't comment on what I was doing so I pretended I was itching my hand, and asked how his class was going.

Bad, he said. Danny O'Mazzi wants to make a bomb.

I laughed and finished with the tree and we were approaching the park now, my mother's tourist office a squat hopeful cabin in the middle. Several ducks, both beige and green, wandered about, tails lifted.

I don't go to movies anyway, I said.

Ever? he said.

Well, I said, no.

That's dumb, he said. That's like not eating dessert.

I smiled. Exactly, I said. I hate dessert.

So what lie is that one? he said. Three? Four?

Really, I said. I have stuff to do. I think it's three, I said. I do need some nails, I said.

Five! he said, smiling back really nicely at me. We crossed the street into the park, lush and well-watered. There were a few people sitting on benches, feeding those ducks.

I have to go visit my dad at the track field, I said.

Liar! he said, without a pause.

I blinked, startled. Helium flooded the air.

Am I right, am I right? the science teacher asked. The movie

theater was across from the park, with BANK ROBBERY! over the marquee in huge puffy black lettering.

No, I said.

Seven! he yelled.

We both buckled over with laughter. It's not funny, I kept saying. My chest was tight with everything.

We stood, poised, on the sidewalk.

It starts at four, he said. Come see it with me. You need a break
too. Let's go. It'll be fun. You can buy me popcorn.

How did you know my dad wasn't at the track?

He shrugged, scratching his chin.

I don't know, he said, after a minute. Sometimes I'm good at
guessing. I always used to bust my parents. How long has it been
since you've gone to the movies, really? The truth, he said.

I hovered on the curb, thinking.

Really? I asked. He nodded.

Three years? I said. Four? Five?

Well Ms. Gray, he said, bobbing his head. You're due.

I backed away toward the middle of the park. I do have to get
something at the hardware store, I said.

He crossed the street away from me, toward the box office. I sit
in the middle, he called.

I waved bye and walked through the park again, in the other direction. I ran through the conversation in my mind: Is your father
at the track field? No, he is not. He's up in an office licking a tar
lollipop. I was running through it all again when, on the east end of
the park, I saw Mr. Jones walk by, swiftly striding, light on his feet,
wearing around his neck, of all things, a 42. The sunlight was hitting his face and he looked younger, brighter, higher, better.

Mr. Jones! I yelled, waving.

He didn't seem to see me. He stopped at the street corner, and pushed the WALK button. Pushed it again. Ready to walk. Walk, walk, walk. Walk, walk, walk, walk.

A woman standing there in a red coat said something to him at the corner, and he nodded, and smiled at her, and made some joke. She laughed. His teeth were long and showing.

The light turned green and he strode off, 42 bouncing on his chest like a rich man's ruby.

He walked past his shop, in the direction of first the hospital and then the highway, but I went to the hardware store anyway. The door was wide open, so I walked in and just took a few nails. Stuck them in my pocket, and left a dollar on the empty counter. Seeing that 42 had left me feeling literally groundless. 42 was a big deal. 42 was leaps and bounds. I'd never seen him wearing a 42 before, ever. Once I saw him at 10 in the morning, leap to 34 in the afternoon, and back down to 17 by evening. He was like the living breathing stock market. And that 34 had been a huge high. I tried to gauge my own mood by his but his always seemed to influence mine: 22? I walked home calm and peaceful. 8? I dragged my feet. If I didn't see Jones at all and his door read CLOSED, then I got a ride home and lay on the living room couch for a while staring at the other objects in the room. I found it difficult to be all joy and humming if when I walked by Mr. Jones he had the 3 on and was lugging out his garbage like a slug. But 42?

I rolled the nails in my pocket and walked out of the store. Outside, the park was quiet and empty. I took my time walking over to the movie theater. The marquee read BANK ROBBERY! and the soap smell was still in my nose, a guard, a big mean bouncer, a slap on the hand, but I took out my wallet anyway, bought a ticket, and went inside.

16

That one boyfriend had a darkroom where he developed the photos he took of rooftops and scaffolding and the occasional one of me naked. I'd sat with him, and once, in the middle of developing pictures, he'd lifted off my shirt and started in on me, two people in the darkest room, smelling of fixer. The black air in the darkroom was way too big for me, I found the darkness to be like a huge black ocean, so in a moment when my arm was free, I flipped on the light and ruined all his photographs. Hey! he said, hey! Jumping back, he dipped his fingers in the fixer tub and lifted up the wrecked image. And there it was, my torso, bleaching out with the light, just dark spots in the center of my breasts, a dark spot of belly button, and then a sheet of white. Look at that, I said to him, it's me.

When I entered the theater, I stalled for a few minutes, going to the bathroom, looking at the candy, reading a review about the movie I was about to see, which said it was action-packed. Finally I walked in, straight down the aisle.

There had been five years of audiences in here since I'd last stepped inside, sixty months of people weeping and laughing at the pictures on the screen, putting hands down each other's pants, or heads on shoulders, or nothing at all—straight up and separate. The room looked pretty much exactly the same. I found Benjamin Smith smack in the middle as promised and took the seat next to him. He turned and his face lit bright when he saw I was there and I felt so good at that I stood, left, flustered, not sure where to go, deciding to buy popcorn. By the time I was back, butter flavoring already seeping over everything, the previews had started and it was dark. I hadn't remembered how loud movie theaters were. I felt like I was inside someone's big loud brain. I passed the popcorn over to him, and twice our hands met in the popcorn bowl and I almost mistook his finger for a piece of popcorn and grabbed too hard and he whispered: Mona, that's my thumb, and I laughed out loud.

He had his arm on the armrest and I put mine on by accident and when I felt his there I moved mine away as fast as I could. He moved his away too. The armrest remained unused for the rest of the movie.

The movie began, grand and booming, and it was about two men who were expert bank robbers. When they robbed their last bank, the job that would make them safe forevermore from money problems, they were caught and sent to jail. There was a scene or two with them in jail, talking about stuff; they didn't seem so bad after all. What happened next was that the city discovered an evil serial killer in its midst and this serial killer tended to leave his victims, coated in money, in banks; the police decided to seek the wisdom of the two seasoned bank robbers, figuring they might be able to help. The police released the bank robbers on the agreement that if they could examine the serial killer's tendencies and solve the problem, they would be freed from jail. I didn't like the scene where the young girl got nabbed off her bike on the way to see her friend, and my eyes were half-shielded by a visor made of my hand when Benjamin turned to me, just tilted his head, speaking the words forward, and said: There's something about you, Mona Gray, that inflates my heart. The serial killer was tying up the woman with white rope. I said: What? very loudly, so loudly that the woman three rows behind us, alone with chocolate mints, said *Sshh* and that made me laugh again because I was nervous. He was facing me now, trying to read my expression, to see if he should repeat himself, and I was praying he would not.

But he'd changed the air, just like that. Now it was different, concentrated palpable, like smoke.

He returned his face to the movie. It was getting more intense: The serial killer was in the darkness of an alley behind a bank, hiding; there was the woman tied up, her mouth stuffed with money; there were two policemen skirting the scene; the two good bank robbers were running to stop the policemen from doing the wrong thing; I couldn't stand it; I decided not to watch, and I closed my eyes and then, like a pop-up book next to me opening, all I could really feel was him right there, breathing, that man. A man. I repeated what he'd said to me in my head. I repeated it again. I repeated it again. On the screen the music was lurching higher, the cellos were speeding up, the strings were vibrating, and I was rising inside; I wanted him to know I'd heard him but I couldn't say anything. My hands were silent in my lap and I began to cloak the air around myself, heavying it, thickening it with aggression and glamour, red velvet breathing, and I made the air seethe off me, onto him, to make him look over again; I wanted to force him to look over just by the power of my will. He kept his eyes on the movie. I thought of him with the bubbles: Did you break it on purpose? Telling Ellen her symptoms. Inflate my heart. I kept my eyes closed and imagined leaning over pushing down the popcorn tub taking his face into mine and then stealing it with a kiss, just like that, we are sealed and joined. Living inside his mouth. Wrapping him up in my cloak. On the screen I can hear a gigantic shoot-out taking place; the bullets are whizzing through the air and burying into flesh and I can even hear the blood, splashing, cinematic, how red and wet blood sounds, and there are the moans—the spare characters are sighing, loud: He got me! And I think of the dyslexic kid in the third grade who is the best drawer in school and how a few weeks before he made me a picture of a horse and wrote on top of it—to Moan—and how I'd oohed over the picture, the mane of the horse, the great proportions, but it made me want to hide, my name up there like that, transformed, just like that, into someone new. On the screen there are shouts and the music is shifting and it's hinting at the sound of resolution, everything is okay now, almost, is it?, yes, it is, you can open your eyes now, but I don't; I can hear they got the bad guy, the woman is freed, the chaos is melting back into order and the woman is leaning on something, comforted by the good cop, or the good robber, just someone good, and the movie music has switched to slow calm strings, it's time for the viola to have its solo, this is the part the viola player tells his mother to listen to, but I keep my eyes closed because I want to kiss him and when you kiss someone your eyes are closed. I won't do it but I want to and he is chewing next to me, the last of the popcorn, cold by now; if he has felt anything from me, he is careful not to show it, and I am wrapped up in myself here, I have cloaked myself, I have sent surges of me over to him, but he knows nothing. He is caught in his own wonderings. He is still watching, he is inside the movie and he is not mine.

17

My mother once told my father that she was taking me on vacation. I can't go, I said, I have homework. I was in junior high at the time. My father brought out his camera, but she waved him off. I wondered what was going on, if we were heading to the city or going fishing or what, but then she told him we'd be back by seven. We didn't even get in the car. Just walked for an hour, past the stores, past the hospital, through empty lots, straight to the edge of town. It was sunset and the air was a bright gold, stretching out, dust particles lit like tiny lanterns. We were silent for a while, and then she said: Mona, out there somewhere is Africa.

We looked at the dry ground ahead of us, the stretch of horizon. It seemed impossible. Even water seemed like a crazy idea. She let out a deep breath.

I want, she said, to take a train through Russia and end up in China and walk through Nepal and pet a goat in Italy and climb a pyramid in Egypt. I want to see the next town, she said.

I just want, she said, to eat a hamburger from a different family of cows.

I kept staring out at the highway in the distance.

I like our town, is what I said to her. I like the movie theater here, how they give you popcorn in a glass bowl.

She put her hand on my hair then, circled it in a ponytail with her fingers, let it free. That's not what I meant, she said to me. I like our town too.

We stood together and she played with my hair until it was dark and the dust turned invisible and we could just see the lights of incoming cars, moving up the highway, passing by. On the walk home we held hands for a bit, which made me feel like her prince, and then stopped at the one Chinese food restaurant and ordered twice as many dishes as we could eat. The bottoms of the huge white bags were warm as we walked the three blocks home, and I held my arms around them, smell rising into my nose: of crisp egg rolls, of brown sauce, of garlic and ginger. At home we spread the dishes over the table in rows.

My father walked over, rubbing his hands together, and I said, We just brought these over from China.

He smiled and rubbed my hair.

I built a tunnel underneath the house, I said. It only takes twenty minutes because it's downhill both ways.

My mom winked at me, sticking a fork into each dish. There were so many choices: beef with ginger, oyster-sauce chicken, garlic broccoli, orange-peel pork. We piled our plates as high as we could manage, to create the whole land in our stomachs, to take the inside linings of our bodies on a visit to countries the outsides would never see.

That night, in bed, shadows moving over the ceiling in dark lakes, I heard my father shifting and coughing. A familiar sound, the settling and resetting of his throat. But that night it sounded like a slow train to nowhere, wind steady and moving through his lungs, always chugging, circling the house, chugga chugga, over and over and over again.

When Benjamin Smith and I left the movie theater, it was just getting dark and the sky was royal blue, the brightness that is post-sunset and pre-night, the air like a dress.

I invited him over to my apartment for some reason. I played with the nails in my pocket—flat head, sharp tip.

We stood in my living room, awkward as poles.

Hey, he said, pointing to the pictures on the walls; I recognize these artists, he said. He especially liked Lisa's row of eyelashed 9's in the grass. According to Lisa, 9's are girls, because according to elementary school art, boys have no eyelashes. In an effort to decorate, I'd plastered my living room with the spiky suns and sky bands of blue of my students—Danny's war where the people shot 7's, Mimi's 3 dog.

I was laughing to him about Mimi, saying something about the way she wrote her name, how she dotted her i's in a new way each week, how this week she was dotting them with hexagons because we were learning shapes, when he leaned in and kissed me, just like that, he traversed the space and halved it, then quartered it, then eighthed it, then shut it down completely until there was no space between us at all and his lips were warm and tasted like butter from the popcorn.

His hand slid under the back of my shirt, palm on spine, strong.

I wasn't sure what was happening. It seemed that we were k
ing. The science teacher, with burns up and down his ar
lips, my hand on his face, on the back of his neck.

Minutes and minutes of this, of his face with mine.

Then I dipped out. Said excuse me; turned to go to the bathroom.

He turned too.

I'm just going to the bathroom, I said.

Let me walk you there, he said.

I laughed at him, his eyes now drooping and earnest, but he stuck by my side.

I'll be right back, I said, in the hallway, by the bathroom door, bleary, closing in again on his face and we kissed, soft, and I kissed his teeth and he smelled like pine and coffee and sweat.

Excuse me, I said again. I'll just be a minute.

I put my hand on the doorknob and I meant to go in, but it was like we'd been drinking magnets. I pulled into him instead, like we'd been sitting at a bar together, finishing off a pitcher of melted-down horseshoe. The longest minute. Is the minute up yet? No, I say, even though the sun is rising now. The minute isn't up yet. I'll just be a minute but I still have a minute left. He put his hand on my cheek and held me there, and we kept kissing, over and over, lips sticking together, my body sealed to his, and I was blooming out of control, and the melting inside was unbearable, and I took myself away.

Be right back, I whispered.

I think you're beautiful, he said.

No you don't, I said.

Panic rose. I knocked on the bathroom door.

No one's in there, he said.

I know, I said. It's not that. He was kissing my neck into cellos. Wait, I said. Stop.

He looked up. I slipped into the bathroom and shut the door

and locked it and confronted my face—pink, eyes bluer than normal. Turned on the water. Took the bar of soap right into my hands. Held it like a slippery bird for a minute and then ran it under the tap. My friend, soap, that small ball of ruin. I washed my hands vigorously, gulping in the smell, and the nausea kicked in right away. I watched my face, watched as the smell heightened the thickness of the longing, then took it away; merged with it, then got big enough to surround and defeat it. I brought the whole bar up to my lips and rolled it halfway inside my mouth, sucking on the white curves, lolling the smoothness over my tongue, drinking the water off the white; I ran it over my mouth, lathered my lips, and I licked the froth off again and again, licked the smooth curve of the bar, reglaze, relick, swallowing it down, forcing the upset, feeling my stomach unravel, rocking back and forth like the autistic kid who came to the school one day and never returned, and Mr. Smith was standing outside the door, I could hear him humming an old-fashioned big-band tune, and when I came out, completely sick to my stomach, he took me back into his arms.

Mona Green Blue Gray, he said. Now your hands are clean.

We walked back to the couch and my body went limp and dead and he was kissing me but it might as well have been nothing then; I was gone. After a few minutes, he looked up.

What's wrong? he asked.

And I said nothing nothing I'm just tired out that's all, and he sat next to me, touching the side of my leg, waiting for me to shift back; he sat with me until the sky dimmed down and the living room was a dark sea with furniture poking up in darker islands. He kissed my fingers. I wanted to shoot him. Blam.

I'm sorry, I said. I'm not into it. I'm just going to lie here until it's bedtime. Please go home.

He took my fingers in his and stroked them down. What happened? he asked.

The air was still and dark, and I could feel myself beginning to blend in with the couch.

I'm just tired, I said finally. I've been tired this whole time.

My heart was thumping, very low and slow. I wished he would get out. I scraped at the oil of soap on my tongue. The science teacher's eye whites were bright in the darkness, disappearing and reappearing when he blinked, and his hand was on my thigh; he wouldn't stop touching me, and it was burning there and I wanted to get it off and I shifted my body so I was all me, alone with the air, none of him on me. Off. Away.

But you were with me before, he said.

I was not, I said.

What happened to you? he asked. Just what exactly did you do in that bathroom? Did you take a pill or something? Come back.

I wouldn't look at him. I couldn't believe he'd said that.

I don't know what you're talking about, I said. Eyes on the pillow. I'm sorry, I said. I just don't want to.

But before—the science teacher said.

That was all acting class, I spit out. None of that was me.

He leaned forward again, but I shrugged closer to the couch, pressing myself into the pillows. Finally, he leaned back.

It was you, he said simply.

The pillows smelled like dust and old sun. I was monitoring my breathing, lungs shallow and vague, heart sluggish, wondering if I'd suffocate, so tight I was against the fabric. I wanted him to get out so I could stare at the 50 and nauseate myself with helplessness. The couch lightened as his weight left it and I could sense the height of him, even with my face pressed against the pillow.

Bye, I mumbled.

Then in the room, his voice, low: Liar, he said, an echo of his earlier self. The delight in the word gone.

The air stiffened. I pressed my face deeper into the pillow. The clock in the kitchen suddenly ticked loudly.

Believe me, I muttered. My head got dizzy.

No, he said. This part is acting class—I give you an A for acting class. But the rest was real. This stuff, he said, this stuff about you I don't like at all.

What am I lying about? I said. I'm not lying, I said.

Stupid Mona, he said, and his voice was one notch louder now. I was here, remember?

The clock was ten decibels louder now, each tick a bomb. I could almost feel the couch pattern peel off my skin. I pressed the pillow against my mouth, a gag, hard, shoving it in as hard as I could to contain what was breaking inside me.

I heard him move away. Turn the doorknob and let himself out. Shut the door. Click. Gone. Quiet. Empty. I rolled away from the pillows, which stuck to my cheek and stomach from the pressure and sweat; it was silent in the living room and I was ready to turn into stone if my heart hadn't been beating so fast; I was ready to turn into stone if I hadn't felt, all of a sudden, like dancing.

I clicked on the light and the room jarred into shades of yellow.

Listen. There was this pretty music teacher who wore red boots and visited school for private piano lessons. On her breaks, she talked about her sex life a lot. Math and music tend to get along, supposedly music is just math in its best dress, so within ten minutes of meeting her, she'd told me how she'd gone out with some man for months and she'd really liked him but then one day announced to him that she only liked women. He was confused for a while and said, Was there space for both? And she said, Nope, it was only women. She meant it at the time, she told me in the kitchen, picking apart a biscuit with her fingers, tapping her red boot heel on the floor in a four count. But, she continued, he never really thought about it, never once said to her: Well what about all those times you were so happy? And what about all those times we rolled around in bed all morning and made pancakes at two in the afternoon? Instead he said: I guess that's the way it goes and I understand, and they broke up. She said it was just weird how certain things were respected without question and if he'd only listened to himself, he might have fought her a little harder. Would you have gotten back together? I'd asked, opening up the refrigerator and closing it again and then opening it again. I don't know, she said. Probably not. But regardless, she said, there is something so awful, something so gross about watching someone who loves you struggle to believe what you both know, deep down, is partially a lie.

18

I didn't talk to the science teacher all week at school. I wanted to staple an apology to my forehead, hold his face and look into his eyes and thank him over and over, but I knew if he touched me again I'd do the exact same thing. I'd be back in the bathroom in seconds, making love to that soap, sticking the soap anywhere I could, just get the human material off.

I managed to see him only twice—once on lunch duty, in a heated debate with Danny. He had more marks up and down his arms, burns riding the split of his sinews.

The second time, I kept my head low. I walked past him in the hallway and mumbled hi and he said hey and that was it.

For Friday, Danny was assigned Numbers and Materials. All week he'd chattered about what he was going to bring, in a vague, excited way, e.g.: I'm going to bring the greatest thing, just you wait! and twice he came over to me at recess to make sure I wouldn't stop him in the middle like I'd done with Mimi. Well, I'd said, sitting on the purple plastic bench, what are you bringing?

You just have to promise, he said, eyes flashing brown and clean.

I can't promise, I told him, if I don't know what it is.

But I can't tell! he said, hitting the bench with his fist. The bench bounced back. I hadn't seen Danny so excited since I'd told him that on Veteran's Day we would be spending the whole class doing word problems about soldiers.

Other than that, since Mimi's 9, things had been uneventful with the second-graders. No one brought any Numbers and Materials during lunchtime, and I didn't really do any fun activities. I was the regular leader of a tight ship. I put names on the board at the first sign of chaos.

Friday morning, Danny stumbled into class with a pillowcase over some kind of large hard rectangle. He greeted the flag as usual, and we did our usual pages in workbooks and even had a quick Friday quiz. I called him up in the last twenty minutes of class. Lumbering over to the front, he placed his item horizontally on the side table. He stared at Lisa and Ann and me for a second, then whipped off the pillowcase, revealing a long case of pale blue glass, frozen inside of which was none other than a left arm.

The famous O'Mazzi arm.

He glanced over at me fast, scared, wondering if I'd stop him.

But I nearly clapped my hands with delight. I'd never seen the rumored arm, had only read about it repeatedly in my mother's *History of the Hospital* brochure. I nodded at Danny, and his face lit up.

This is my dad's arm, he said. It's kind of like a big 1.

He lifted it on its side, vertical.

The class was totally silent, staring. Ellen drew in her breath in a thick heave. Danny kept glancing at Lisa expectantly, but she was quiet and seemed impressed. Ann had her arms folded. In the bottom right-hand corner of the glass, I could see the fancy engraving that read FIRST SURGERY.

I'm so glad you brought it in! I said. Danny beamed, all ready to start with the subtraction when I told him that today for a change how about trying some multiplication. His face lit even more; Lisa made an enraged sound from her desk. Danny picked up the glass case, and hugging the bottom he held it as high as he could; inside, his father's arm was slightly bent, with the palm half open in a vulnerable kind of way, like a bud crumpling out to the sun. 1 times 88 is 88, Danny said. There was a tan mark where his father's watch had once been, and a neatly sewn-up shoulder. I saw no sign of blood.

What's 1 times 156? I said. 156, he said, shifting the weight of the arm on his knee. 1 times 387? I asked. 387, he said.

Your dad has hairy arms, said Ann from her chair.

It's not fair that he gets to do multiplication! said Lisa. All the other kids were shifting in their seats, and Ellen's face was whitening by the minute, so I told her to go use the bathroom because she tended to pee when upset. She left quietly but I heard her run as soon as the door shut.

What's 1 times the world? called out John Beeze.

The world, said Danny O'Mazzi.

He balanced the arm again on the table by the chalkboard and showed us where it was cut off at the shoulder. My dad got stuff in it in the war, said Danny. But it only got really bad in the hospital. He spent the first night of anyone in there, before the elevator even worked.

Does your father use a wooden arm now? I asked.

No way, said Danny. He's no cheater.

Elmer raised his hand. Can he eat? he asked.

Danny rolled his eyes.

Does he have cancer? Lisa asked. No, she answered herself.

What war? I asked.

Danny shrugged. The one, he said. In another country.

The whole class nodded sagely, so I didn't press it further.

He did a few more multiplication problems, and then stood proud next to the arm, a small sergeant with his glass flag, when Ann raised her hand.

Yes Ann? I said.

I don't think it looks like a 1 at all, she said. It just looks like an arm. I don't think it should count for Numbers and Materials.

You should talk, said Danny, gripping the glassy blue corners. So far I've brought in a stick 11 and a gelatin 4 but you haven't brought in anything all year except that bad 3 of nothing.

Ooooh, said John Beeze.

Kids, I said, walking to the board.

Well, I have something today, said Ann, voice priggish, as if it were the most normal thing ever.

I raised my eyebrows. At the table, on a piece of scratch paper, Lisa was writing out her multiplication tables at a breakneck speed.

I have a great number today, said Ann. I really do. It's way better than that arm that is not a 1.

Ann, I said. Cut it out. I put her name on the board: Ann.

Danny, I said, thank you for a terrific addition to Numbers and Materials.

I'm done? he asked.

I smiled. Do you have anything to add? I asked.

He put his arm around the arm. One times a million billion trillion is a million billion trillion, he said.

Very nice, I said. Maybe the rest of you can look more at Danny's dad's arm at recess.

Danny nodded, smug. I led the class in a short round of applause, and he returned to his seat where he stuck out his tongue at Ann.

Enough, I said. Lisa stopped writing, and put down her pencil.

Then Ann DiLanno stood up.

So can I go? she asked. We still have ten minutes, right?

You really have a number today? I said. A solid number?

She glared at me. I'm not a LIAR, she said. Of course I have one. I have the best one of all.

I leaned against a bookshelf.

We hadn't had a peep from Ann since the 100 of rhinestones that I still was irritated about, and which turned out to be stolen. It belonged to some old lady who baby-sat Ann and her sister on Thursday afternoons.

All right Ann, I said. Show us what you got.

I waited for her to wave her arms and produce another 3, this time made of noxious gas from science class, but instead she walked straight over to her blue backpack and very carefully unzipped it.

And . . . here . . . it . . . is! she said.

She raised her arms and held up a 42 made of wax.

See, she said. Look. Look at this perfect number I brought.

It was about the size of a tennis ball, hanging from a dirty string. I recognized it instantly.

Isn't it beautiful? she said.

Bo-ring, said Danny O'Mazzi, clutching the blue glass arm.

Now. As much as I was supposed to be the same to all my students, I wasn't, and Ann had made me annoyed first by the 3 and then by the fickle rhinestone 100, but far more than any of that, most of all, I did *not* like seeing that 42 separate from its obvious owner.

Where did you get that? I asked, sharp.

I made it, she said. Out of beige crayons.

There are no beige crayons, said Lisa.

Ssht, Lisa, I said. Ann, I know you didn't make that. I know who that belongs to, I said. Here. I'll give it back today.

No, said Ann, hugging it to her. It's my number. I brought it in. I made it out of beige crayons. There are too a lot of beige crayons. I want to do some adding and subtracting and multiplying with it, she said.

Lisa held up her page with all the problems and cracked it in the air. No multiplying allowed, she said.

Ann took a deep breath. $42 + 1 = 43$, she said. $42 + 0 = 42$.

Okay, I said. Now—

$42 + 6 = 48$, Ann said.

Good adding Ann, I said steadily. This number belongs to my neighbor. It's very important. Where did you find it? Hand it over.

She clung to it. $42 + 3 = 44$, she said. Now, subtraction. $42 - 1 = 41$.

She got one wrong, said John Beeze.

That's all fine Ann, I said. Now, I'd like the 42 please. Numbers and Materials is over for today.

Danny was carefully pulling the pillowcase back over his father's amputated arm. The rest of the kids were stirring in their seats, restless. 42 was too tricky a number to get really involved with. Lisa was out of her seat now, standing at the supply cabinet, holding up a pack of crayons.

See, she said, sorting through. Red, green, blue. None of these are beige, she said.

Ann held the 42 tight to her chest.

$42 - 0 = 42$! she said. What do you use to draw bread? she asked. What do you use to draw potatoes?

Ann, I said, trying to keep my tone calm. You're right, good point. Lisa, sit down. Those things are beige. I need the 42 please.

But I don't want to give it to you, Ann said, words rising.

I use brown for bread, said Lisa. I like wheat bread.

My voice leveled out. Ann, I said, have you ever been in the hardware store? Where did you find it?

Ann clutched the 42 closer.

I found it in the park, she said. Under my pillow.

And I use gray to draw potatoes, Lisa continued, from across the room.

I found it in my dinner, Ann said. In the mashed potatoes. All *beige*.

That's a lot of mashed potatoes, said John Beeze, impressed.

Come on, I said. It belongs to a man named Mr. Jones.

I know Mr. Jones! piped in Ellen.

Good, I said. Well then you know that he makes these numbers himself and he needs them. He absolutely needs every single one of them. Lisa, come back and sit down.

Ann clung to it. I love 42, she said.

I hated seeing it get dirty and melted from the warmth in her arms, and the string was old and fraying and I had just seen it bouncing on Mr. Jones the other day, a grand permission slip for the universe. His face lifted, eyes clearer than usual, skin brighter, with light inside it. And I couldn't stand to think of it gone, of him waking up and feeling exactly precisely 42 and not being able to locate his mood and searching and searching but finding only 41 or 43, neither of which was quite right, not quite right at all, and having to drop down to the thirties, having to settle for something lower because he couldn't announce it exactly.

Lisa walked back to her chair, making popping sounds with her mouth. John was in a thoughtful stupor, thinking about how big the plates must be at the DiLanno house. I held out my hand. Ann glared at me.

My 42, she said, twisting with it. It's perfect, she said. It's not like that dumb arm that doesn't look like a 1 at all.

Danny stood up. My arm is great! he said. My arm is number one! My dad fought in the war! he said.

I'm not kidding around Ann, I said.

The bell rang for recess. Half the class ran out. Danny stood, taut and peacock-like for a second, and then picked up his 1 and hauled it away. Lisa hung around by the door. Ann remained in her seat, firm.

I found it in my ear, she said.

Lisa pulled in her breath. That is gross, she said. Can you hear me? She raised her voice. Helloooooo, she said.

I sat across from Ann.

I have an idea, I said to her. Why don't you go to the hardware store with me after school. That's where he works. We can give it back together then. He'll be so happy you found his missing number. Maybe he'll even give you a reward.

Ann's eyes were shifting around the room. I was trying my

hardest not to grab the 42 out from her lap when she wasn't looking. I didn't want to risk breaking it.

With you? she said.

With me, I said.

Today? she said.

Today, I said.

But I have ballet lesson at 4:30, she said.

We'll go right when school is out, I said. That's plenty of time.

Okay, she said. Her face had been hard with determination but it softened a bit now.

I found it on my front lawn, she said. It was there waiting for me, just on time. Right there hanging from the front tree. It was perfect, she said.

42.

You found it on your front lawn? I asked.

Exactly, Ann said. Right on the tree in the middle of the front lawn.

The seat I was sitting on was wood and I reached my hand down and knocked on it then. Because Ann was 8. It was highly likely, it was almost ridiculously possible, that one of her parents was 42. I couldn't even stand to ask right then; I just wanted to get the number back to Mr. Jones and be done with it. My stomach unsettled itself, fearful.

Can I go? asked Lisa from the doorway, above the sounds of screaming students getting their snacks.

Sure, I said to her. It's recess.

No, I mean to the hardware store, she said. Can I come too?

I looked at Ann. She waited for a second and then gave a shallow nod.

Fine, I said. We'll all go at 3:00 and you can all meet Mr. Jones.

Until then I'm wearing it, said Ann, standing up. She put the string around her neck and stood there, defiant. The number fell to her belly button, slightly distended under her red T-shirt.

Be very careful, I said. 42 is a good number.

It's six times seven, Lisa said from the doorway.

It's how old my mom and dad are, said Ann, running out to the yard for recess.

19

I had gotten one postcard from Joanna Stuart, my old neighbor, now in Florida. She smeared sand all over it and glued it on the card and sent it to me because I had begged her for one before she left. Look, I showed my mother—Florida. We put our noses up close to smell the sand which smelled like glue. My mother hung the postcard in her office. On it, Joanna had written: Hi Mona, I live in Florida, Bye.

They'd buried the baby here. I visited it sometimes, when walking around town, a quick detour through the cemetery, patting the grass and dirt, pretending I was Joanna. Hi baby, I said to it, this is your big sister here. I figured it wouldn't know the difference.

The headstone was the same size as all the others. It was the only one with that last name.

Lisa, Ann, and I entered the hardware store at 3:20 that afternoon, after a difficult walk from the elementary school through the park. The girls clambered over the benches and tree roots, fast and

nimble, playing some pirate game made up clearly by Lisa, who
was the bad pirate and was persecuting Ann, the slave pirate. Ann
wasn't happily playing along. Whenever she said, Let's change
games, Lisa said: Ohoy! Bad pirate wants to change games! Three
hundred lashes with a whip! And that was the end of that. Ann finally retaliated by telling Lisa that her hair was beige. No it is not,
Lisa huffed. My hair is called dirty blond. I use a *yellow* crayon to
draw it, she said.

I didn't intervene. I had no chalkboard to put names on. I only
asked Ann once if her parents seemed okay and she didn't understand the question; I shook my head, worried, grazing tree trunks
with the edges of my knuckles.

When we reached the street, I asked Ann and Lisa to hold
hands to get across. They refused for a few minutes and we just
stood there, stuck on the sidewalk, and finally I agreed to let them
touch elbows, faces turned away, like a mean-spirited country-
western dance. We crossed and then walked into the hardware
store, bells signaling our arrival. I looked to the cashier. Mr. Jones
was not at the counter.

Ann and Lisa were sniffing down the aisles.

Doorknobs! Lisa cried out, holding up one of blue glass.

Ann was peering in the bin of iron nails and gently dipping her
hand inside as if it were a tub of water. I looked to the empty spot
on the wall where my ax had been.

Mr. Jones? I said.

There was no sound or movement anywhere.

I guess he's not here, I said.

The girls weren't listening. Ann was putting a flashlight to use
and spotting the walls with circles of white light, jiggling them into
squiggles and lines and pluses.

Lisa had a knife out.

Put that back, I said.

She curled a smile at me, coy.

NOW, I said, my voice harsh, and she hung it back on the wall. Ms. Gray is mean, I heard her whisper to Ann. Ann giggled.

Still no Mr. Jones.

I went over to the place where my ax had been and just stood near it, still loving the space it had held, visiting its absence here in the hardware store. Ann and Lisa were back to the pirate game and Lisa was telling Ann she was going to staple her to a shower curtain.

Mr. Jones? I called out, again.

Mr. Jones, said Lisa.

I have your 42, said Ann.

I have your 42, echoed Lisa.

There is nothing on earth more annoying than a kid doing echoes.

Stop the echo, I said. I heard a tiny, barely audible Stop the Echo from Lisa. I glared at her and walked to the back door, looked around, but still saw no one.

Well, I guess he's not here, I said.

I found the girls at the rack of hammers.

Get away from those, I said. You know, you really shouldn't come into hardware stores, I said.

Ann is a human nail, said Lisa. She needs to be hammered. You brought us here Ms. Gray, she said. Hey, Ann, bend your head.

Lisa lifted a huge hammer off the wall. Ann, not thinking, bent her head. I pulled Lisa aside. What is going on? I hissed.

She wouldn't look at me. I don't know, she said. I'm in a bad mood, she said.

I took the hammer out of her hands and stuck it in a pile of pliers.

Is your mom okay? I asked.

She hardened visibly. Get away from me, she said.

I found Ann standing solo by the drills. I'm going to keep the 42, she said. He's not here. Finders keepers.

Ann, I said, he'll be here any minute. I don't know why he isn't here. Maybe he's getting a cup of coffee or something. Are your parents healthy? I asked.

Lisa went and stood by the door.

I'm going to count to five hundred by twos, she called out.

Great idea, I said, relieved.

And then, unless we are leaving, I'm going to go get hit by a car, Lisa continued. Here I go: two, four, six . . .

Ann's fingers were gliding up to a drill.

My parents are healthy, she said. My dad said he needs a drill.

That's good, Ann, I said. But you'll have to come back.

I want a drill, she said. The owner isn't even here, that's his fault that he's not here. No one would ever know.

No way, I said. Come on.

Fifty-two, fifty-four . . .

Okay, how about one nail? she pleaded. Can't I have one nail?

They were loose in the bin, little tiny T's. Dark brown-gray.

So I can hang up the 42 on my wall? she asked.

But you're going to be giving the 42 back, I said. Remember? That is not your 42. Remember? Mr. Jones! I called. Are you here?

One hundred and twenty, Lisa said, loud.

Ann kicked her feet around. I don't know what you're talking about, she said.

Ann! I said.

Her face soured. Fine, she said, I'll give it back.

Then you can take one nail with you, I said. But just one.

She spent what felt like an hour picking out the perfect nail, named it Howard, and walked over to the door. Still no sign of Mr. Jones. Lisa was on the verge of finishing up and I hurried Ann toward the exit and Lisa shouted, Five Hundred! but by then I had my hand firmly on her shoulder and she pretended to rev up to run into the street into the cars but I held her back, hard, and said: Don't you even DARE, in a really mean voice, and her shoulders sank and she moved closer to me and suddenly became very lov-ing. We walked through the door, and the sun was a notch lower, and in the park kids were out of school, jumping around the benches, flicking the drinking-fountain water.

I'm supposed to go to the hospital now, said Lisa, taking my hand.

Ann said: I'm supposed to go back to school and get picked up for ballet class.

Want to switch? Lisa asked, as we reapproached the park.

Sure, said Ann. Okay.

Lisa's face lit up. Really? she said. Really?

Ann burst out laughing, total revenge exacted for all the pirate suffering she'd endured in the last hour.

No way, she said. I was only kidding.

After I'd dropped Ann in front of the school and Lisa in the blue pooling reflections of the hospital, I went back to the hardware store to look for Mr. Jones. The door was still wide open, and the room filled with evening, shadows of tools shifting on the walls.

Mr. Jones! I called out. Are you here? Hello? Everything was quiet, still. I went into the back room, piled high with brown boxes and the sawdust-sweet smell of broken cardboard and old apples, but there was no sign of him. Mr. Jones? I said again. I was feeling worried by now, he'd never been gone for this long from the store when it was open, so I walked over to his house, and knocked on his door for a good ten minutes. There was no answer. I needed the feeling of knocking on that fine oak so I stayed there for a while, just working out my whole day on the door, my worries about Ann's parents, about Ann taking the 42 from Mr. Jones, about the approaching end of 50, about a tableful of coughing seven-year-olds, about Lisa's mother stuck on the sixth floor of the hospital for the rest of her life, about the science teacher's smile, the way he saved it and didn't overuse it, and I knocked until it was too cold to stay. I waved at my parents' house on my walk home. I didn't go inside.

part three

42

20

I had my first big success in track as a fifth-grader, and in fifth grade speed is a big deal. I was faster than the fastest boy. And he was fast. On that particular day of sprinting I really felt like I might kick into orbit, thigh up shin back heel high blast forward. During the race, seeing those other kids next to me, ahead of me, behind me, made me want to run faster just to leave them behind, just to race ahead like nobody's business, and that's what I did, and I was nothing but tight muscle and intent. When I won I was the most famous girl of all girls for a while, and the boys started insulting me and I knew that was good news and I ran again and I ran again and I sprinted again and again until it was clear that I wasn't one-shot lucky. That girl can run, said my gym teacher. I went and stood at her hip. She saw I was there. You can RUN, she said. I felt like I might die with pride for myself and die of humility because I didn't know how I did it, I just did it, and it made me want to give things to other people and I shared my dessert at lunchtime and when I came home from school I helped my mother lay out her brochure on *History of the Highway* and I thought secretly who needs a highway really when we all know I can run to New York City and back in five seconds.

Excuse me, I have someplace to go.

I ran track in high school for a year and I got it back for a bit, for a second I felt that crack-open of my lungs, releasing new lungs, infant-pure, a new heart, shuttling out from behind the old one, new bones, air shedding the skin off my back, molting and sleek, but my father had faded by then, and it never tasted as good as that one time before when I won and I *wanted* to win. That weekend, he and I went to the track so I could show my stuff, and he had the stride of a giant but still called me Miss Speedy and one time, once, I almost pulled ahead.

At home, I stood on top of the dinner table. I am growing right this second, I told my mother. She laughed at me. Really, I said. I think I can feel my bones move.

She poured me a glass of milk. Here, she said.

We both watched the white liquid disappear, from the glass, into me: magic.

Birthday 51 was now a week away.

The nothing birthday. The number of nothing.

Sunday, I grabbed the plant food to give my dad but walked downtown first to check on Mr. Jones.

The hardware store was still wide open, but there was still no sign of him perched on his stool by the cash register, reading. Rows of hammers lined the walls, hard black worker hats on wooden worker bodies. I called his name and looked through the store again but no luck, so I left, unsettled. On my way out, I picked up a lug nut from the bolt bin and popped it in my mouth, sucking on the metal, sticking my tongue inside the ridged hole.

I headed over to my parents' house.

Halfway there I spotted a tree with a beige tumor on its root. I would've passed it right by, not even noticing, sometimes trees have tumors on their roots, wondering where is that Mr. Jones, but as I got closer, the tips of the roots formed into angles and lines until my eyes focused and I saw that it was a wax 13 on a string, nestled at the base of the tree. My heart stopped for a second. I spit out the lug nut. Bending down, I picked the number out of the dirt and hung it from my arm. What did this mean? I stroked the hard wax. I kept walking, worrying that this was some kind of message from Jones to the world, not sure what the message could be, when I turned the corner and crossed the street and saw, strung on the side of a hedge, a solid wax 8.

The edges of my skin shook into ice. This was wrong. This was not right. Behind me, some adults pushing a perambulator rolled down the block. When they turned the corner, I ran to the hedge, picked the 8 up carefully, warm and yielding from the sun, and unhooked it from the brambles. I held it for a second: 8. A bad mood, a short life. Then hung it next to 13.

Over the next five blocks, I found more numbers, let loose like stray dogs, my heart shaking each time I saw that dirty string and angled glob of wax swinging off the back of a bench or hanging from the branch of a tree. 23. 37. 4. 11. All levels. All types.

Ages and moods and deaths spread everywhere.

I collected each necklace carefully, brushing off the dirt and hanging them over my arm. Where was Jones? Decaying on a beach? Starving on the highway? I slipped 23 over my head, wax bouncing against my ribs as I walked. I waited for a sense of harmony, but the truth was I felt much lower than 23, maybe more at about 10, and so it seemed false to advertise the wrong number and therefore disrespectful to Mr. Jones's system. I took it off.

I tried knocking on his door again but no one answered.

At my parents' house, I found my father in the backyard, on his knees, trying to pat down the grass that had not yet grown back from his failed *Shape of Health*.

How are you doing? I asked. I was wearing beige. I knelt beside him, and handed over the plant food.

He was ripping up dried blades. I could still see the open circle clearly, brown and distinct, the broken part of the arc filled with green grass.

My father pulled out a few more handfuls, then put a palm on my shoulder. Thanks, he said, squeezing. He reached in the bag and sprinkled bits of plant food, like fish food, right on top of the burn marks.

Nice to see you, he said. What else you got there? He looked at the tangle of wax and string on my wrist. I waited for him to recognize the numbers, advise me on what to do.

Numbers, I told him, raising my arm slightly.

He nodded, agreeable, and then stood and walked forward to the sliding door, back into the house.

Mr. Jones had lived next to my parents now for over twenty years, grading my math tests and advising on plant food, but there hadn't been even a flicker of recognition on my father's face.

This is a man's heart, I said, quietly. I am holding somebody's heart right here.

We both went into the living room: me with that diary on my arm, my father sinking into the sofa; I called out a greeting to my mother, who was in the dining area, working. She grunted. I asked her if she'd seen Mr. Jones around town this weekend; she said no, come to think of it, and asked why. I said no reason. Air felt thin in my nose. My father wrapped himself in a blanket even though it was warm in the house, and clicked on the TV. He spent a few minutes resetting his throat while we sat together on the couch, flipping the channels around, finally settling on some sepia action movie. It was yet another bank-robbery story, but he seemed to be enjoying it, and there were the bank robbers together running and there was the heiress with her long dress and long lashes and there were the guns and bam-bim-boom, commercial. I missed the science teacher hard, watching it.

How's school? he asked.

There's no one in the hardware store, I said.

My father put his feet on the leather footstool.

What do you need? he said. Toolbox is in the garage.

I petted the wax of the numbers. I don't need any tools, I said.

He straightened the blanket over his legs. I wanted to know how he was doing, in a real way, but I didn't know how to ask. Instead, I reached into the shelves over our heads and brought down the scrapbook of him running, him young, the black-and-white photos of a man who had not been black-and-white then. I looked at the ribbons, ran my finger over the curled satiny old blue. First place, first place, first place.

Do you miss running? I asked.

First place, second place, first place.

The show was back on. Now the cops were in on it. Now they were all chasing each other in their cars. Race race race. Cops turn. Robbers turn. Screech and lean. Corners. Everything was very fast. The actors were of another time, with different bone

structure, wider foreheads, wavier hair. My father didn't say anything until fifteen minutes later at the next commercial and then
he just turned to me and said Yes.

I forgot what I'd asked and then, against my will, remembered.
I tore a piece of plastic off a scrapbook page when I realized what
he meant. I wanted to see what it would take to get him to move
fast—A gun? A bomb? Me? I'd dash past him, lap the block four
times, cheeks red from exertion, alive! alive! panting, done by the
time it takes him to walk to the doorway and watch me go.

I closed the scrapbook, which smelled faintly of mildew by
now, blew some dust off its cover, and replaced it on the shelf next
to the skin-disease books. The TV show was back on and I said bye
as the sound of gunshots rang out. He smiled at me, closed his
eyes. Afternoon was getting to him. I adjusted the numbers on my
arm and went to say good-bye to my mother, who was immersed at
her desk with photographs of snarled jungles next to clean text in
white squares.

She worked steadily and I stood over her, watching. She
matched up the corners and lines. She drew the glue stick neatly
along the backs of the papers.

You know, I said finally, no one from here is ever going to go to
any of these places.

The yellow light from the lamp made her face yellow and she
looked up at me, eyeglasses on the bridge of her nose. I felt mean.
I waited for her to yell. I was wishing she would yell at me, her rude
daughter, pack her bags, and prove me wrong, come back with defeated snakes curled up her forearms in scaled bracelets and a tan
of dirt, her legs all fine thighs and lean savvy calves.

All she said was: So.

21

Monday morning at school began normally.

I made myself a cup of peppermint tea in a dented steel mug, and brought it with me into my classroom.

The night before, I'd stored the wax numbers I'd found on some towels, nestled like jewels on terrycloth. That evening, I'd called all the Joneses in the phone book—there were twelve—but no one knew where he was and a few people didn't even know who he was. One number had a different area code and I could hear cars and trucks in the background while I talked to the old woman, Mrs. Hilda Jones, living the last of her life in the big city. What's his first name? she asked, in a rickety voice. I had no idea. Minehead? I ventured. Minehead Jones? She said no and have a good night dear, and when we hung up, I missed her. I missed the sounds of those trucks in the background, people out driving the grid of the city.

At school, I sipped my tea and worried. The first grade was on a field trip with the reading teacher to some reading festival so I had a little extra time before the second grade marched in.

Benjamin walked by once but it was too fast for either of us to say anything. I was staring at the door, formulating a vague plan of what to do if Ann did not have the 42 with her, when a group of parents entered MATH without knocking.

They were all talking at me before I could even say hello.

I recognized most of them. They seemed to be the parents of my second-graders. I thought, first, before I could understand their words, that they were citizens for Mr. Jones, that they knew about the 42 and the other numbers, and had put together a search team, bless them. Or I thought maybe they'd found Mr. Jones, and then I wondered if they were going to tell me how Ann DiLanno's parents had both died in a freak dual poisoning accident, and then I worried about Lisa's mother and then about my own father but finally my ears tuned in and heard what they were actually saying.

—and besides it is flat-out in-ap-pro-priate to teach math using severed limbs, said Mimi Lunelle's mother, her mouth loud and pink, fingernails flashing bright as a beverage. Mimi dreamt all weekend that a gigantic 1 was coming to strangle her, she said. I mean really. Whatever happened to buttons and blocks?

Severed limbs? I said. I took a sip of my tea.

Mr. Gustav Gravlaki's mustache trembled from the tight pursing of his lips.

We will not have Elmer doing mathematics with arms or anything else that has to do with war! he yelled. Mrs. Gravlaki jumped in agreement, wearing her housecoat, a blur of red buds and orange suns. Yeah, said another parent standing behind.

I remembered the O'Mazzi arm then, that hopeful flower of a hand reaching up to the ceiling through the pane of blue glass, and felt confused and tired by their distress. I'd been so upset by the 42 that I'd forgotten all about the severed arm.

Did it break? I asked feebly.

No, it did not *break*, said Mrs. Lunelle. Don't you get it?—It's frightening for children to look at body parts in their math class!

They loomed over me, righteous. I raised up from my seat and stood near the chalkboard.

Well, I said slowly, trying to clear my head, I feel it was a good learning tool. In fact, it was our entryway into Multiplication and Divison. This is a very advanced class, this second grade, I said.

They shook their heads in unison, leaning toward me—furious, but also tentative; everyone is secretly a little afraid of the math teacher. All you really need to do is write $100,000 - 56,899$ on the board, and people will flee in droves, horrified by the sight of all those zeroes in the minuend.

I was about to launch into a speech about gratitude toward war veterans when my boss, luckily, bustled in, wearing a green suit that looked more like Wednesday than Monday. I felt off schedule just looking at her. I stopped talking; I had very little to defend; I thought the severed arm had been one of the best Numbers and Materials all year. What you people really need to worry about, I wanted to say, is that Mr. Jones from the hardware store has vanished and could be caten by coyotes somewhere and that there are death numbers strewn all over this town.

My boss took the group outside to talk them down and then the bell rang and inside trooped the second grade, all seven in a row, greeting their parents, bewildered, delighted.

What's happening? asked Elmer. Why is my mom here in her kitchen clothes?

Nothing, I said. Don't worry.

I shut the door behind them. Okay class, I said. Take your seats, don't worry about the parents—

So are you busted? Ann asked. They're never here unless you're busted.

They sat right down in their chairs, expectant, except Ellen, who stood at the pencil sharpener, sharpening the second end of her pencil so it had two points and looked something like a hammerhead shark's hammerhead.

Ann tried to hear the discussion outside, but all we could get were low urgent tones. I was relieved to see that she looked like she'd had a normal weekend.

It's because of the arm, said Mimi Lunelle. I had nightmares all weekend.

Danny's eyebrows drew in. My arm? he said.

Ellen, said Lisa, I can't hear, will you stop sharpening your pencil already?

It's not *your* arm, Ann said to Danny.

Lisa had her hand over one ear. Whose parents are here? she asked.

Oh, said Mimi, everyone's.

I interrupted to ask who had brought a Number and Material for class today but no one had; it was Monday, they admonished. I put some hard subtraction problems up on the board. $15 - 9$. $23 - 16$. The kids didn't move, and Ellen remained at the sharpener, *rrrrr*, noise whirring on, then off.

Lisa fidgeted in her seat, and after a minute, stood over Ellen, poked her shoulder, said, Stop it!

Flip. *Rrr.*

All weekend, I'd thought of Lisa, going to the hospital after wanting to get herself hit by a car, standing and looking at tubes and pumps and quiet machines. The lure of a death that is fast and loud.

Outside the room, the parents were still in a heated, indecipherable discussion. Ann had her ear to the wall, eyebrows scrunched. Flip. *Rrr.*

I can't hear a thing, she said.

Lisa twitched, still standing, and then dragged a chair to the bookshelf, stood on it, and lifting high on the balls of her feet, reached up and pulled the ax down from its hanging place on the wall.

Let's get the dumb parents really mad, she said.

Lisa, I said, don't mess with the 7.

It's not a 7, said Ann. It's a hatchet. It never looked like a 7, ever.

Put down the 7, I said. I walked over and plucked it out of Lisa's hand.

The parents are not dumb, said Mimi Lunelle. My mom is really smart.

Flip. *Rrr.*

Oh Ann, by the way, I said, did you bring back the 42? Did anyone happen to see Mr. Jones from the hardware store this weekend?

Ellen's lead broke and she gave a gentle sigh and stuck her rapidly shrinking pencil back in. *Rrr.*

Lisa stood directly next to me and gripped the handle of the ax in my hands.

Hey Lisa, Ann said from her seat. I have an idea. Ms. Gray, she said, let's make a Number and Material out of you.

The class hushed, instantly.

What do you mean, Ann? I asked.

I mean, I bet you won't cut off a finger if we dare you to, Ann said.

Oh, I thought to myself, I bet I might.

Lisa leapt in. We'll cut one off you, Ann, she said. I'll come over and chop off your big mouth if you don't shut up. Ellen, STOP sharpening!

John Beeze, always loyal to Lisa, started laughing. Ellen, at long last, removed her pencil from the sharpener, blew on it as sweetly as if it were a dandelion wish, and sat down at her seat. Without the electronic *rrr* buzz, the room seemed almost empty now, it was so quiet.

Ann looked a little nervous but still turned to me. Her eyes were clear and green. Who cares about a finger? she said. Let's make a 1 for Numbers and Materials. It'll be way better than the arm.

Hey, shut up, said Danny O'Mazzi.

It's true, Ann said, holding up her hand, splaying her fingers. Look how straight, she said.

Well, Ann, I said smoothly, I need my fingers to count on. Fingers are a crucial part of math because ten is a good base. Nine is too complicated. Our bodies are made for math, just the way they are, I said.

Don't do it, said Elmer.

I shook my head. Don't worry Elmer, I said. Lisa, let go of the 7. Class, pull out a piece of paper and do the problems on the board. Remember to carry over from the tens place if you need to.

Ellen removed a paper from the stack on the bookshelf, and wrote her name and the date at the top in perfect cursive. She had no eraser but then pulled from her pencil case a second pencil, this one with no lead but just two sides of eraser, hammerhead shark's brother, that she had constructed herself with some tape.

Come *on*, said Ann. I want to see a finger as a 1.

I want to slice Ann in half, said Lisa, still standing next to me.

Danny O'Mazzi pulled off his sneaker and sock and stuck his bare foot on top of the table, wiggling his toes. Yesterday in the bath I thought my baby toe looked kind of like a 6, he said.

I got pulled in for a second, looking at it. His toe did look kind of like an upside-down 6, or else a little wobbly 9.

So chop if off then, Ann said.

You can stick it on your mantel, added Lisa.

Danny whisked his foot off. Lisa and Ann shared a rare smile. Outside the room, the parents laughed about something and heels clicked away from the door.

Dumb parents, I hate them, Lisa said.

Just because you have none, said Danny, pulling on his sock.

John jabbed Danny in the side with his elbow. Lisa's mouth got hard and she raised my hand with the ax, trying to pull it up, get under the chair and swipe at Danny's toe, but I pushed her fingers off, placing the ax down on the side table where I held it down firm with my hand.

Stop! I said. Let's get going. Ann, did you or didn't you bring back the 42? Danny, stop smelling your sock.

Elmer's eyes were wide and nervous. Is skin a material? he asked.

Everything is a material, said John Beeze.

Lisa was still standing right up next to me. I could feel the heat of her, rising. This room of mine had no windows.

If you want someone to cut off a finger, I'll do it, she said then. I can do it. I don't mind. I want to do multiplication with 1 like Danny did. We never get to do multiplication and I know all multiplication, even the 9's. I want to play an amputee in Life Acting class.

It was MY idea, said Ann. That's not fair.

Lisa, I said, no way. Go sit.

She stepped closer to me, skin so warm I could feel it. Why not? she asked. I don't even *like* my fingers. They're stubby. See? Give me back the 7. I want to be a word problem. Lisa had five fingers and then she cut off one finger. How many fingers did she have left?

Four fingers! sang out John Beeze.

Now Ann stood. Well I want to too then, she said.

I pressed my hand on the ax handle as Ann approached, ready to go hang it back up, and Lisa was glaring at Ann and Ann was glaring at Lisa and just then, at the back of the table Ellen, surrounded by hammerheads, peed.

Ellen, bathroom, I said.

She crept off, but in that one instant, Lisa had seen my fingers relax and she whipped the ax right out from underneath my palm.

Now she was swinging it around the room.

Hey, I said. Lisa. Hey, put that down, NOW. Lisa!

I put her name right on the board: Lisa.

She ran to the back of the room, face alive with light. I ran after her.

No, she said. I want to do it. I want to try. $9 \times 9 = 81$, she said.

Ann was pouting and jumping. It was MY idea, she said. I want to, I want to. It was MY idea. Lisa always gets to do everything!

Lisa was dodging and jumping, off chairs, under the table, around the bookshelves. I tried to grab her, putting check marks on every chalkboard I passed, one check, two checks, three. She didn't even look up. I went left. She went right. More: four check marks, five check marks, more than anyone all year long, six check marks, seven, benchtime for the whole year, Elmer gasping at the

rows of checks on the boards, but Lisa wasn't even paying attention. She dodged again, and then, eyes glittering, put her hand flat
down on the back table, and the ax hovered wobbly above it and I
was rushing over and everyone was watching, frozen, and the ax
swooped low and slammed down, bang, just missing her hand by
an inch to make a dent in the fake wood, which shook slightly from
the blow. My heart nearly stopped and Lisa was staring at her hand
which was all there and John Beeze had pulled the ax out of the
desk and was trying to give it to me when Ann rushed over and
swept it from his hands.

   Mine! she said.

   Lisa was still looking at her hand, all whole, in total dismay. I
don't need all these fingers, she said. I wanted 9 to be my base. I
wanted one less.

   I grabbed Lisa's hand in mine and pressed down on it, dizzy
with relief. Then Ann yelled out: I want two less, I want five less,
and Lisa wrenched free from me, not done at all, and said, Then
cut off your whole arm then, I'll cut it off for you, it was not your
idea, it was MY idea, and I yelled at Lisa to sit down and the rest of
the kids were now either cowering in corners or running around
the room in frantic scurried movements and someone, maybe
Mimi Lunelle, was under the table, and Elmer was muttering
under his breath something religious, and I managed to get closer
to Ann but she held the ax behind her and I didn't want to touch
her because the blade was lined up with her back so I yelled SIT
DOWN in my shrillest authoritative voice and most everyone sat
down except Ann and Lisa, like gargoyles posted at two corners in
the far back of the room, Ann with the ax behind her, Lisa's hands
in fists.

   I held out my arm, palm up. If I don't get the ax right this second, I said loudly, I'm calling your parents and having them come get you. And Ann, I need the 42, too. Hand over the ax.

I knocked on the real wood bookcase.

My mom is dying in the hospital and can't come get me ever again, said Lisa.

Ann's face screwed up. Lisa ALWAYS has an excuse, she said. She held tight to the wooden handle. I'm keeping the ax. And I'm keeping the 42 too, she said.

Those are not yours to keep! I said. I moved sideways, very slowly, to get behind her so I could grab it.

Ann, Lisa said calmly. If you give me the ax I'll cut off your fingers for you.

No, said Ann, in a sour voice. Ms. Gray, can I cut off your finger?

No, I said, getting closer.

Ann held the ax up over her head. Then I'm going to throw it across the room, she said.

No! shouted Mimi, Elmer, Danny, and John.

But Ann already had it pulled back, deep behind her. I was almost in grabbing range but she was fast, reaching up and out, arms weighted from the steel, preparing to throw it, fling it across the room, and her arms lifted over her head, but right before the ax could leave her hands and go flying, the weight forced the blade down, curling the length of her own body and hitting straight into her bare thigh. We all heard as it cut past the skin, and cracked into the femur. Dead on. Metal on bone. Burying its blade in her flesh— hard into soft. Square into cylinder. Ann DiLanno, inside coming out; Ann DiLanno, opened up like timber. Blood filled in around the blade, fast. The skin puckered open and Ann's face transformed into a horrified grimace and she began shrieking.

I've cut my leg off, she screamed.

Oh no no, I said, just a little part, and Lisa was at the tissue box pulling out tissues one after the other, *ssh ssh ssh*, and I could hear Mimi gagging and Ann was crumpling down to the floor, the ax sticking out of her leg and right then Ellen walked back in the classroom in a new pair of pants, those ones left in the lost-and-found for just that purpose, plaid pleated pants of another decade, but when she saw what had happened, she turned on her heel and walked right back out. Lisa pulled the ax out of Ann's leg, which spit blood once unplugged and we lay pieces of tissue on the open wound which was like using a bottlecap as an umbrella, and I tried to pinch the two sides together but they kept pursing open. Ann was sobbing. It was a thick gash, a clean line, a ravine of blood, from above her knee straight up her leg, closer to inner thigh than outer, far far too close to everything important, and it reminded me, all too clearly, of a version of the blow I had almost given myself.

It's just a cut, I said, my hands shaking.

It's a One, said John Beeze, sitting in his chair.

One times Ann is Ann, said Danny O'Mazzi.

22

It was Ellen who made the call, rushing from the room to the phone and punching in 911, picking at those plaid pants, pointing to the math room before the laughing parents, now sitting in the kitchen gossiping, even got wind of what had happened.

Then they rushed in.

They found Ann in a heap by the back table, dizzy, choking with sobs, her thigh laced with wings of tissue, drooling blood out of her leg.

Mrs. DiLanno entered, face emptying, scooping up Ann, saying, Baby are you okay? Baby what happened? Is she okay? Call the ambulance! and the sound of the siren could be heard approaching closer, the one ambulance in town, jaunty and clean, red light awhirl, and Ann started to cry louder in response. Lisa had her cheek shoved against the wall.

Elmer's father ducked through the doorframe. I didn't know where to stand, where to put myself. The ax was on the floor, blade red-caked, and Gustav Gravlaki picked it up by the handle, boomed: And what is THIS? He brandished it up high, until it grazed the ceiling, and he looked like a painting, holding my ax, the exact muscled mustached woodcutter. I couldn't meet his eyes. My boss rushed in, and ordered me to go sit in the kitchen and wait for her, which I did, head down, looking at no one. I could hear the rest of the second grade running outside and getting ready for recess early and Lisa was making her popping sounds and I could hear Ann crying and crying and Mimi was crying and Elmer was crying, talking about the bone, how he heard the bone, how it sounded like a rock, and Ellen had apparently peed the second pair of pants and there were no more pants in the lost-and-found so she had to wear a shirt as a skirt, sleeves hanging off her child hips like tentacles. John was dribbling a kickball. Lisa stopped by the door of the kitchen and looked in at me. In the background, we could hear Ann's voice shaking down in metered sobs.

You shouldn't be talking to me, I said to Lisa. Go to recess now.

The ambulance siren arrived, no Doppler effect because it did not pass, but instead stopped, parked. Kids from other classes rushed to the windows to watch. Word got out fast: Ann cut off her leg, Ann killed herself, Ann killed the whole second grade. The paramedics busted in; Lisa didn't move, didn't look. She was very used to ambulances. Big deal, she once told me. It's a white van. Two huge men in huge outfits ran inside, bright blue and ruddy, the sons of proud mamas, fellows who knew CPR and used it, who birthed babies and put the air from their lungs into the lungs of wheezing town members, who watched people breathing in the park, in the hardware store, in the movie theater, and recognized their own breath in the lives of others—these men ran inside like health embodied, and the kids pulled away from the windows, leaving opaque ghosts of noses and mouths on the glass. I heard scurrying and adjusting as Ann was lifted onto a stretcher and carried out; she went by my door, bloody, wailing, getting drawings piled on her by the art class in session who all suddenly became very generous with their art and put them on her belly like sacrifices: Here, Ann, a pony; Here, Ann, a flower. Papers that weren't steady fluttered to the floor. As she exited, I heard Ann wail, through her sobs: This doesn't look anything like a pony.

The low voice of a paramedic. The opening and closing of the school doors.

She was followed by the parents and then the kids after the parents and then the siren. Then quiet. Elmer crying. John dribbling that kickball.

The rest of the kids started to trickle into the playground. I had my hand flat on the seat of my wooden chair, pressing down, harder, and put my head face down on my other arm, slumped on the table in the kitchen. I could hear my boss shooing away all the remaining kids, telling them to go to recess. I heard Danny O'Mazzi ask, Is Ms. Gray still here? and I felt a rush of love, sweet biceped Danny. An ax? somebody else asked. Can I have Ann's cubby? asked a third.

No More Questions! my boss said loudly. Go play, children!

I heard the science teacher, releasing his group, talking to a fifth-grader, voice worried, asking what had happened, asking where I was, but my boss swept in and told him if he didn't do recess duty right that instant he was fired.

That's three, I thought, vaguely. I almost laughed out loud because it was not at all funny. I wanted to see him. I wanted to tell him he was right, every time, he was always right.

I heard my boss click off to her office, feet sharp and fast and angry on the tile. The school quieted.

I breathed in the familiar smell of my skin. The thought of Ann in that ambulance, bleeding on a stretcher, made my ribs compact into a box; my breathing was thickening and I thought I might throw up when I heard some kind of shifting sound and picked my head up to see Lisa still standing outside the door, small and tight in her little shorts and shirt, staring at me. Lisa Venus. Wearing the I.V. that first day like a queen. Her eyes were wide and direct.

Well, she said, I guess we killed her.

You're not supposed to be here, I said. You should be going to recess now. You're late.

Behind me, the refrigerator whirred. The room was half-dark. I was thinking about Ann saying, That's not from nature, that's plastic, about Lisa's zero—funny Ann, sensible Ann, cut-up Ann the cutup.

Then after a second, I took in what I'd just heard.

Wait, what did you say? I said.

Lisa knocked her hips from side to side. She looked perfectly reasonable. She said: I took down the ax and you brought in the ax. We can send secret messages to each other in jail.

Ann's not going to die, I said.

Lisa's voice was an afternoon breeze. And, I took the ax to the back of the room, she said. And, I told Ann to cut off her whole arm. And, I hate Ann, she said.

She's not going to die, I repeated.

She is TOO going to die! Lisa said, her voice rising. Fingers clenching into a fist.

I felt like going to sleep right then, and put my head on the table, closed my eyes. What kind of math teacher keeps weapons in her classroom? The insides of my eyelids were warm and dark. I could barely hear Lisa.

Ms. Gray, Ms. Gray, she was saying, and I ignored her, kept my eyes closed, willing her away, get out, go play some murderous pirate game on the playground, go enslave Elmer who's probably throwing up himself somewhere from the sight of blood, the sound of bone, and I thought she had left and was sinking back into my deep worm-infested pit of horror and shame when I heard in the background a very familiar sound, one so familiar I thought I was doing it myself until I realized my hands were still. Just a simple tapping, the most familiar sound in the world to me.

Knock knock knock. Inhale, exhale. Knock knock knock knock. A perfect replica.

I opened my eyes. She was still standing there in the doorway, intent, her fist now on the wooden door frame. She kept knocking.

Look here, she said, lookie here, I'm Ms. Gray. Look at me, I'm Ms. Gray. She knocked at exactly the same rhythm I did. She kept knocking. Knock knock knock knock. She drew in her breath just like I do. It was a very effective imitation. I wanted to knock, watching her be me, knocking.

I kept my head on the desk, eyes on her steadily.

Knock knock knock knock.

Lisa, I said.

Her face was flushed with focus. Sometimes, she said, I do you for Hands-on Health. After cancer. If there's time.

I pressed my hand harder on the wood of the chair, bothered.

I'm not sick, I said, into the crook of my elbow.

Lisa kept knocking. The dull clamor of recess rose outside.

My eyes felt tired against my arm, barely working, watching Lisa knock that door frame. I thought of Mr. Gravlaki waving the ax in the air, his face dark with rage, and panic flared in my ribs.

Ann, I murmured then, mostly to myself.

No, said Lisa, Lisa.

I kept watching her. Inhale. Knock knock knock knock. Then exhale. Repeat: Inhale. Knock knock knock knock. Exhale. Perfect.

I didn't know you knew I knocked, I said then, slowly.

Lisa shrugged. Everyone knows, she said. Even Mimi knows and she barely knows anything. When I do you for Guess Who? in Hands on Health, everyone gets it in about a second.

I kept my hand on the chair. Rubbed knuckles against the wood. Guess Who. I'd thought I'd been carrying on my knocking secretly, my own guilty private guillotine. Since Mr. Jones and the day of the makeup math test, no one had ever said anything to me about it.

Does Ann know? I asked, starting to close my eyes again even though my heart was beating faster.

Lisa shrugged. Dumb dead Ann, she said. She just thinks you're weird.

The school was bone-silent now except for the sound of Lisa and the ticking of the clock in the hallway. Tick tick tick. Knock knock knock. I slumped there, head on my arm, listening to her be me. I tried to fall asleep and could feel myself almost drifting away, lolling off, pushing away the morning, redoing the morning in my head, trying to calm that flower of panic that was folding then re-blossoming each second, a kaleidoscope of movement and small-ness, fold, blossom, a fist, a rose, but after a few minutes, the knocks on the door frame started to intensify, each a little harder than the last. The knocks became hits. Pow. This brought me back. I opened my eyes.

I don't do it like that, I said.

She didn't respond and I watched her pull back her elbow and pound a fist into the door frame.

Hey Lisa, stop, I said from the nook of my arm. Go to recess already. You're really late.

No, she said, I'm keeping you company. She drew back her arm again as if to sock someone and lobbed it into the wood. Her fist made a thudding sound. KNOCK KNOCK! she yelled out. I lifted my head from the desk and half sat up. I wanted her to go away, to stop being there.

Lisa, I said again. Stop it.

She looked over, eyes shiny. We glared at each other and then she pulled back her arm and struck her fist into the door again. I could hear the skin on her knuckles grating against the wood, the way the sound absorbed instantly, no echo.

She smiled at me. I didn't smile back.

She drew her arm back again, far.

Come on! I said, sitting straight now. STOP IT. Go away! My God, haven't we had enough bloody children for one day? I said. Go to recess, Lisa!

The rest of the school was completely quiet, drawers and cubbies, floor and cabinets, all silent watching wood.

She nodded right at me this time, eyes bright as dimes. I slumped back down, partway to the desk.

She turned back to the doorframe.

Hands at your sides, I said.

She did that. She kept her hands at her sides. She stood still for a second and I thought we were done. I waited for her to leave the room, cawing, to run out as fast as she could. To disappear. She moved a step back. That's when Lisa spun out.

I didn't expect it, but I should've; she was standing there tighter than normal, standing with her four feet of self, that's it, that's all you got, said God, that's all I'm giving you to contain it ALL, and she had this blank look on her face and I was back to my elbow, still watching, about to close my eyes again when she gritted her teeth and in the center of a second reared her head back, and before I even knew what was happening, hurtled it forward and slammed it with all her might into the hard wood of the door frame. And before I even knew what I'd seen, I heard it, heard the shatter and bash of her skin and skull, the weight of the blow, and her forehead split open, broken continents, bleeding. She had some kind of giddy dazed woozy look on her face and I stood up, suddenly, shaking, awake, heart slapping, and I might've done nothing but stand there and shake if she hadn't reared back again, ready to bang forward again, crush those continents into countries, crush those countries into states, make more space in those four feet, it's just not enough space to keep all of it in, and she started arcing forward, eyes focused, but this time I leaned in and seized her, got her by the shoulders, her body hot and slippery as a fish, closing my arms around her, tight, pinning her own arms down, one across the other, so she was hugging herself.

Let me go! she yelled.

Her hands were flailing, trying to get free. I held her down. When I spoke, my voice was sharper and clearer than I expected.

I don't want your company like that, I said, hard.

She drew her head forward and slammed it back into my chest, ramming it hard so it clipped me on the chin, socked me with the weight of her cranium, and I could feel the breath knock out of me for a second, feel my sternum bloom open and bruise, but I held on even tighter, and she tried again but this time I clamped a hand down on her forehead, palm on her skin, wet now with blood, mashing her head into the nook of my neck.

She was kicking up her legs, thrashing around like a drowning man.

Knock knock! she yelled into the empty school. Who's there? she yelled back. Ann! she said. Ann who? Ann Chovy, she said, and she started laughing, loud and joyless: Ha! Ha! Ha! she yelled. Ann Telope! Ann Esthesia! she yelled.

I was holding her as hard as I could, one hand on her forehead, pressing down on the broken bloody skin, spit flying out of her mouth, my other hand clamped around her waist. She was giving off heat like a radiator. I could hear the sounds of recess growing outside, screaming kids and cement and rubber balls.

Give me some wood, Lisa said. Get me near wood. Her voice was high now, rising. Give me some Ann Esthesia, she yelled. Oweee, she said. Now you're going to get FIRED, she said. No more math class. Her head was bucking but I kept my hand hard on her forehead, pressing down, her whole brain, her small skull. She kicked her legs up higher and harder. And by the end of the summer, no more mother, she said. And soon a new math teacher and Ann is going to be going to the school for kids with no legs.

Ann has legs, I said then, meekly.

Lisa kept kicking and thrashing in my arms and she swallowed and it turned into a gulp and I could feel her whole body starting to shake. She was twisting so hard I was getting rope burn on my inner forearm but I held her strong, I had her, she was not going to break free, and she yelled, Let me go, and I didn't say anything back this time and she kept wriggling and thrashing and yelling: Let me go! Let ME GO! Come on! I *want* to be one of the bloody children, I want to have cancer too, I want cancer NOW! and she was twisting and twisting but I kept holding her as tight as I could, fierce as a vise, and she said: I wanted to cut off MY arm, I wanted to do it, how come Ann got to do it, how come Danny's dad got to do it, how come Ann got the ax, I wanted to bleed all over the carpet, I want to have chemotherapy, I want to have no hair, I want to be in the hospital too, she's going to have to die all by herself, and she swallowed again, ragged and raw, wheezing, and the trembling was like a whole town on fire, the shaking up to the sky, smoke over the sun, her body rabid with shaking, unstill, blurred, and her breathing was thick, and it was my turn to talk but I kept holding her close and I had nothing to say, there wasn't much I could say to that. No matter how many times she kept her mother company, it was clear who was leaving, and who was staying put.

23

One Sunday I remember, I am standing in the kitchen, watching my father make his lunch for Monday, spooning dim hard-boiled eggs into plastic bags. Made by yellow hens, once. The day is foggy and dull but I go to the garage anyway and pull out my bike, ride down the street, ride. There are a lot of people on the block, the curbs are filling up with cars, more cars than I'm used to, red cars and blue cars, cars from all over town, people dressed in black walking slowly up to the door of the Stuarts' house. And then I re-member, of course, it's the funeral today, today's the day they bury the baby in a coffin the size of a suitcase.

Biking down, the wheels are moving over wet pavement, mak-ing shushing sounds, and I look at the rows of people lined up in front of the Stuarts' house to give their condolences. I ride by, watching, turn at the end of the street, ride back. Only Mrs. Finch had died on the block so far, and she did it with the grace of an old woman, slipping off, calm and natural. Old Age on the chalkboard with Ann's > next to it. Old Age is a whole different story; on her lawn, the 84 was a triumph. Biking past the Stuarts' house, I look at the rows of black-coated men and black-skirted women walking

up the walkway and everyone is solemn and the casseroles are covered with fogged tinfoil, steam rising through the cracks, smelling
of green vegetables, of orange cheese. A row of dishes on a red-
checkered table. Everyone is hungry.

I ride by and look at the faces, and all the faces are drawn, away,
stricken, and this is from the going of a life most people had barely
even met, a baby who couldn't speak yet, who never knew the name
of her mother, who never even walked but spent her whole time on
earth with her back to it. I'm riding, wheels turning, puddles spinning off the rubber, thinking that the people all stand together
with their faces so death-heavy because it's backward. Because it's
in the DNA to collapse at the sight of a coffin the size of a suitcase.
You don't want to pack your baby on a trip like that. When you walk
down the street, and you happen upon a baby carriage with a baby
inside it, and you peer in the blue awning, the scalloped edges, the
squirmy flesh inside, there is one simple given: If all goes right,
this baby will live in the world longer than you.

It is all about numbers. It is all about sequence. It's the mathe-
matical logic of being alive. If everything kept to its normal pro-
gression, we would live with the sadness—cry and then walk—but
what really breaks us cleanest are the losses that happen out of
order.

I was fired that afternoon. It was swift and clean, done inside two
sentences. My boss opened the door, said I was a wonderful math
teacher, but she never wanted to see me again.

Lisa had been picked up by the second ambulance of the day,
no siren. She knew the paramedic. Hi Sue, she said, as the medic
walked in, tall in her blue outfit. Oh hey Lisa, Sue said. What you

have there on your forehead? By that time I had her lying down, holding an ice pack to the broken skin, her face puffy and red from crying, eyes woozy from the blow. I watched as they walked to the van. Lisa settled in the front seat, strapped herself in, flipped down the mirror on the sun visor, and investigated her forehead. There was no expression on her face.

I walked home very very slowly. The few blocks took forty minutes. A man was out on his lawn with a hose, watering those iron geese which made a plinking sound. A few parents drove past me, on the way to pick up their kids; it was close to that time by now. I didn't wave when they tried to catch my eye through their windshields. They'd find out soon enough. And stop waving. Halfway there, hanging from one of the lampposts, I saw another one of Jones's numbers: 7. I picked it up, broke off the wax awning so it looked more like a 1, and slipped it over my head. I felt better, wearing that home. I felt clear. Once back, I took out the trash, slow, moving my body as minimally as I could. I didn't talk to anyone. I thought only about Ann in some room with a doctor sewing up her leg like a sweater; I thought only about Lisa, the ridiculous warmth of her in my lap, heading to the hospital, another one of the bloody children now, her forehead a map of continental drift. Trying to push out of her head like my father with his circle in the backyard, push it away, push it off, break a hole in the forehead and maybe the bad stuff will just seep out, like smoke unraveling from a bubble.

I sat in front of the television unmoving for over four hours until there was a knock at my door.

Perhaps it's the police, I thought mildly. Welcome officer of the law. Come on in. I imagined the chilly bite of the handcuffs. Right then, I loved the idea of jail. It seemed so organized. No rent. No cooking.

But instead it was Benjamin Smith the science teacher, standing on my welcome mat, looking taller than normal, face handsome with concern. His arms, as always, covered with burn residue. I felt a surge of something, seeing him. He said he'd heard the news and was very sorry. You're a great math teacher, he said. I said thanks but I deserved it. I asked if he'd heard anything about Ann and he said apparently she was getting twenty-seven stitches (and to my own horror all I could think was that's the first odd cube, three times three times three, and not a bad number for next year's math class, multiplication), but he said they thought she was going to be fine even though she'd lost a lot of blood. They're going to keep her in the hospital for a bit, he said. Tomorrow they'll see if she can walk all right. I guess she split down the bone, he said. My chest halved, hearing that. He told me Lisa was staying with Elmer Gravlaki's parents for the week and that she had a concussion and had gotten four stitches on her forehead and a huge bottle of pain relievers to carry around but she wasn't staying overnight at the hospital and instead said she was going to audition for a maraca player in a band with her pain reliever bottle.

A concussion? I said. I could feel the shaking start.

She's walking and talking, he said. She's okay, he said.

I touched my eyelashes with my finger. They were gluing together.

He fiddled with his watchband. Really, he said.

My fingertips were getting wet. I'm sorry, I said. Thanks for coming to tell me. That was really nice of you. Sorry, I said. I wiped my finger on my sleeve.

I saw her, he said. She's okay.

Looking up for a second to nod, I caught a glimpse of his body hidden inside his shirt, his clavicle, straight across, good bones, this man: a man.

Then it's his lips, on my lips, I'm remembering, I can't help it, and I'm thinking of the backyard with the bubbles, and how it smelled there, all thin soap and thick smoke, and how he caught me cheating, cheating to lose, and how when he said that, I could've ruined him with gratitude, tore him down, tractored him over, that he could catch me, thatIcouldbecaught.

Lisa insisted I come see you, he said. I wasn't sure if you'd want a visitor.

I looked back at the ground. The mat on my front step was made of fake grass, and when I rubbed my foot over it the blades leaned and popped back with the vigor of plastic.

I'm glad you came, I said.

She says hi, he said.

It was a horrible day, I said. Tell her hi back. She's all right?

She's not even staying over at the hospital, he said.

He shifted his weight to the other foot. He was still standing at the doorway. I asked him in but he said that was probably a bad idea. He congratulated me on getting fired first, and we both laughed sad short laughs.

I could feel, almost against my will, the magnets beginning to charge, to circle around each other, each magnet spying the other magnet. I see you, one body says to the other. He was standing there and I was still staring at the plastic mat, Ms. Gray the math teacher, destroyer of children, and I told him then that I was sorry about the other day. You were right, I said, I was lying. He nodded. I thought of Lisa, heavy in my arms, heavy with the weight of every-

thing, like layers of lead slid carefully under her skin in a new epi-
dermal breakthrough, and I took a breath and told Benjamin the
science teacher that next time, if there ever was a next time, if I
said I was going to the bathroom, he shouldn't let me go. He
coughed a little. The words were out, floating around the air.
Words so big to me they blocked out the sky. I rubbed my foot over
the grass mat. I felt like I was praying. He said: Ms. Gray, I am not
your bathroom monitor. I smiled a little at that. I know, I said.
You're right, I said. But just once, I said. I could hear him breathing. On the street, someone honked. I said too, louder, that maybe
it was good if Lisa pretended to have cancer some of the time because otherwise she pretended to have cancer all of the time. When
can I see you again? I asked, down to the floor. The sentence
knocked around in my mouth like a hard candy. My magnet was
moving forward but my body kept still. I could feel the pull, dark
and thick, and he said he'd come by to check on me in a few days.
Really? I said. Yeah, he said. That would be really great, I said.
Come before Sunday, I told him, it has to be before Sunday. I think
I can come Saturday, he said. And please tell Lisa, I said, that I'll
check on her soon. Okay, he said. I lifted up my head. I had been
talking mostly to the floor the whole time. It took every bit of myself that was there, slogging up from the depths, but I put a hand on
his arm. Good, I said. He looked at my hand. We both looked at my
hand.

24

I spent the next two days in bed. I knew the school schedule by heart and on the minute, imagined the kids shifting from class to class, facing their math substitute, Elmer back under the table, Danny coated with rubber bands. No Ann. A zero next to her name in the roll book. Absent. Lisa with angry stitches all over her forehead, telling the younger kids she got them by banging against the wall as hard as she possibly could because she wanted to see what it felt like to break open your head. Shaking her maraca of pills, and dancing.

The art teacher called to say it was too bad, some parent called to yell, my mother called to remind me that we were all going to dinner that Sunday night for my father's fifty-first birthday. I almost laughed out loud, that she'd told me which birthday it was, just in case I'd forgotten. Ah, I said. 51.

I stared at the 50, unfolded on my bed.

On day three, I tucked the 50 in my pocket, picked all of Jones's numbers off their nesting spots inside my towels and hung them carefully off my arm, in order.

I left my apartment and walked downtown.

The movie theater was still playing BANK ROBBERY! which made me walk even slower, and the hardware store remained OPEN but empty. I didn't see any more loose numbers, but by now lots of merchandise had been stripped from the aisles. I counted twelve missing hammers and a bunch of missing buckets and one of the clocks on the wall was gone. There was a trail of red licorice on the floor of Aisle Three. I asked some pedestrians on the sidewalk if they'd seen Mr. Jones, but they seemed preoccupied and all of them had shovels or pliers in their pockets.

Isn't he from the stationery shop? asked a woman with two wrenches poking out of her purse.

I shook my head and held up my arm, but she didn't stay long enough to see. The wax numbers hit against each other, friendly.

I wandered until the shadows turned my skin aquamarine, which meant I was at the foot of the biggest building in town, and it occurred to me that maybe he was in there and that's where he'd been the whole time: sick. Pulling open the glass doors, I entered the lobby, air tinged from the tint of the transparent walls. The pale fishlike nurse at the front station told me there were five Joneses in the hospital, but three were women, one was a child, and the fifth, she said, was a visitor from Nebraska who'd stepped on a nail.

She beamed at me. Anything else? she asked.

My fingertips brushed the strings on my wrist. As long as I'm here, I said, do you think you could you tell me an Ann DiLanno's room number?

She checked. DeLanno, she said. *D-e?*

D-i, I said.

Di-Lanno, she said. That'll be 907.

I took the thick-cut waterlike elevator to the ninth floor, an underwater dive upward, blue windows rising, stomach falling, floor after floor, sick people in cubicles, a spot of sun in the center of each pane of blue glass.

The doors opened and I stepped onto the floor, which buzzed with coughing and coffee and low voices and bings, and I walked the hallway, slow. 901, 903. Muttering how sorry I was. 905. The door was white and the number was brass.

907.

Heart pounding, knuckles pressed to the door frame, I edged my face forward, peering in, but Ann's bed was a tight empty ship, and a nurse with a turquoise bow tie strode by and told me Miss DiLanno had checked out late that morning.

How's she doing? I asked, but he'd already turned the corner to tend to someone else's broken something.

I stepped into Ann's room, with its boxy metal machines and I.V. standing by itself. There was one flower left on the floor, a limp daisy missing half its teeth. I looked out the window but the glass distorted the ground so I just saw a few dark rectangles that were benches and the messy blobby tops of trees. A person came in with blue window cleaner and squirted it on the blue windows. I held Mr. Jones's numbers close to my body.

Back at the elevator, I pressed the Down arrow and a man in a suit waited with me, and when it came we both got in and I pressed L and he pressed 6. We dropped three easy levels and then the doors opened to the sixth floor. A huge sign faced the elevator that said CANCER WARD, in dignified type on a panel of brass.

The man in the suit walked off, into.

I stood and looked at that brass panel.

Elevator doors are polite. They do not rush you. They accomodate last-minute decisions.

The Cancer Floor didn't look how I'd imagined. Most people had hair, and the tiles were white in the light, and the magazines in the lobby area were about cars, of all things. I'd wandered only three doors down when I came to the one that said VENUS on the chart.

I wasn't prepared to say anything so I walked past, fast, first, and my peripheral vision found a person inside, a splash of red, a TV on.

I circled the floor.

I passed the magazine lobby, the nurse station, passed the elevator and the bathrooms. Most of the room doors were open and I walked by a boy making blanket sculptures on his bed and two women in nightgowns standing at the window. I walked by an old bony woman in the middle of a rigorous phone call, and a man playing checkers against himself. I could see the Venus door approaching from a mile away and slowed down the closer I got. One step. Two steps. Three steps.

I didn't look in. I walked right by.

The boy's bed sculpture was the ocean now, blankets rising and cresting in waves, and one of the women by the window was trying to get the stain out of her nightgown. The bony woman was gesturing wildly with her bony arms to the phone. The man had reached the end of his board and kinged his red checker.

As a kid, I spent a lot of time looking in my father's medical books on skin disease. They have pages and pages of color photographs. When I had friends over, this was usually a place we ended up—stuck behind the living room couch, eyes squinted, book open, daring each other: I bet you can't handle 135; kiss page 257, and I'll give you my dessert.

Mrs. Venus's door approached again.

I walked very slowly. Turned my head as I passed the open frame. I saw the wig on her head, so bright it looked like a teenager's first experiment with hair dye. She was laughing at the TV. Her eye whites were not clear.

Straight ahead. Keep walking.

Lobby. Bathrooms. The elevator doors opened but no one came out. The bed sculpture now included a ship of the boy's pillow. The standing woman had a hand on the stained woman's shoulder and both were bathed in blue light. The bony old woman lay quietly in her bed, phone inert. She coughed. I stopped and looked in.

She turned her head. She had thin wisps of white hair like bleached grasses growing off her skull.

She coughed at me.

Hello, I said.

She didn't say anything. She coughed again. It wasn't a big dramatic cough like the ones I'd been hearing all month at school. It sounded more like dry paper flapping against a cactus.

How are you feeling? I asked.

She rubbed the corner of her eye and flapped the cactus again. There was a pitcher of water on a table near her feet.

I walked in. She muttered something under her breath.

Inside the room, I could hear the machines clicking and sighing, busy at work. She coughed a few more times and put a palm protectively over the glittering rings on her left hand.

I filled a glass from the pitcher, and the water stained as if chlorinated from the light coming off the window.

She watched me, sniffing a little, but she didn't reach for the glass. Her fingers trembled, stroking the sheets, hardened filaments of bone. There was a bunch of flowers across from her, a lot of tall yellow ones and fat pink ones, and a balloon in the shape of a bird that said FLY HOME SOON! She was hooked up to an I.V., a heart monitor, and a metal box I didn't recognize.

She scraped out another cough. I brought her the glass. She didn't move her fingers to take it.

Who the hell are you? she mumbled, coughing.

I stood there with the water.

What the hell are you waiting for? she asked.

Lifting the glass to her lips was hard because her head was so low. The water flowed out, horizontal, dribbling into her mouth and down her neck. She coughed. Sipped again.

I wiped her neck with my sleeve. Mr. Jones's numbers grazed her shoulder.

Stop that, she said.

After her fourth sip, she cleared her throat and asked me again who I was.

I'm just the math teacher, I said. Her neck was drenched.

They're sending me a math teacher now? she croaked, incredulous.

No no, I said. I'm Lisa's math teacher.

Lisa? she said.

I'm visiting, I said.

Thank the Lord, she said. I hate math.

She took another sip of water. I watched the green line of the monitor make mountain ranges of her heartbeat. When she'd drained the glass and I'd half-soaked the pillow, she said: Scram, and turned on her side in the bed.

I did the rest of the floor very slowly. The man playing checkers was beating the pants off himself. I finished in the magazine area and just stood and watched the open rectangle that was Mrs.

Venus's door. I sent a hello on the air to her. I could hear the laugh track of the TV from where I stood.

When I pressed the down arrow for the elevator, it opened right away, and took me back to L.

Growing up, I knew those skin-disease photographs by heart. I'd dare myself to look at them, even when I was home alone, but every time the page opened to a person covered in warts, arms so swollen they looked like overstuffed furniture, dot-to-dot faces, breasts lost among larger hives, genital catastrophes, each time I looked I felt the same rush. My friends screamed and ran from the room, but I stayed put. Brought my lips to the page.

25

Once out of the hospital lobby, I walked into the white sunshine and went straight to a bench. I knocked for a bit, but the wood was weak and mealy, so on the way home, when I passed Mr. Jones's house, I went back to his front door, and knocked and knocked, pounded that fine heavy oak. I needed it, and I knocked just as I always did, in sets—inhale, knockknockknockknock, exhale. Inhale, knockknockknockknock, exhale. The numbers bounced under my forearm.

I kept going, still knocking, red wigs, still knocking, but even on this good wood, the knocking wasn't working very well.

I couldn't stop hearing Lisa's imitation, her knocking that door frame with me.

I do you, she'd said, for Hands-on Health. After cancer. If there's time.

I kept knocking, but it almost seemed funny, and I kept going, waiting to see if I could shake the image of her, rapping her knuckles on a table, standing in front of the science class, hands waving in the air. I know! I know! they all yell. Me, in the other room, putting away folders, thinking I could spin myself out privately.

I was trying to get back the release, still knocking, realizing this meant the science teacher knew too, still knocking, when all of a sudden the door opened.

My hand fell forward. I'd been so absorbed with the knocking part that I'd completely forgotten this was a door at all.

Standing in front of me, with slight stubble on his cheeks, eyebrows turned in, wearing a 15, was Mr. Jones. Not bloody at all. Whole and annoyed. My heart ripped up at the sight of him, his lucid stare, his mighty dimensional eyebrows.

What is going ON? he said. My God, I've never met a more persistent knocker in my life. What the goddamn do you want.

I stared. I wanted to touch him, push him. He wasn't dead. I felt my mood lift, double, triple, at the sight of him.

Are you selling something? he asked. I should call the police on you.

Mr. Jones, I said. Where have you been? Mr. Jones!

He started to close the door on me. I don't want anything, he said.

Wait, I said, it's Mona Gray. Don't you remember?

Remember? he said. Remember what?

I thrust my hand inside the doorjamb.

I have your 42, I said. Or one of my math students has it. She was in the hospital. It's my fault. We brought it but you weren't there. People are stealing from you. I have your 4, 8, 11, 13, 23, 37, and 7 as well. Except the 7 is broken. What happened? I said.

I wedged my foot in the door frame and held up my arm. The numbers moved below, wax wind chimes, clinking and thudding beneath my wrist.

Don't you want these? I asked.

He glanced down and his one visible eyebrow lowered.

Look at that, he said.

It's almost your whole year, I said. Where were you? I've been so worried! The hardware store has lost a ton of merchandise. Someone stole the clock with the authentic blue glass cover.

He stuck his eye closer to the open crack of the door frame.

I was on vacation, he said.

Vacation?

Vacation, he said.

You were on vacation? I asked. You left your store open.

His eye looked right at me, eyelashes thin and widely spaced.

I was 42, he said. Who gives a damn when you're 42.

I thought of him on the street that day, the light in his step, the rubies in his walk. Glorious notorious uproarious 42. My permission slip into the movie theater, into the science teacher's mouth. Wait, I said, don't you remember? I grew up next to you. I bought the ax? I said, stomach balking.

He blinked the one visible eye.

I bled on it, I added. Ann's leg floated up in my mind.

He shook his head. Ruins the blade, he said.

The blade is ruined, I said. You were on vacation? Also, I knocked on wood in your math class, I said. Do you remember that?

No, he said. I remember no Monas never.

I felt bad. And odd. And suddenly very unimportant. According to my memory, even though he'd ignored me at the hardware store so many times, I'd still figured or hoped he'd once had an altar to me in his living room because I was the best noticer in the land, and I'd imagined that whenever he saw me his heart had risen with pleasure until I spoiled it all for him at age thirteen and then he'd had to rip down the altar and mourn the loss of me for weeks—the only woman who'd understood him.

Perhaps, he said, you used to sell me cookies?

I looked at the ground, which read WELCOME.

Never, I said. Never mind. We used to know each other.

I was about to turn on my heel and leave when he opened the door a crack wider, and his one eye became two.

Thanks for collecting my numbers, he said. That was very thoughtful. But I don't need them, he said. I'm making a new batch today.

Now that he'd said it, I could smell the wax, the piquant aroma of candle making coagulating behind him.

He reached down, touching the numbers I'd brought. His current choice, Old Reliable, the very scuffed wax 15, clinked gently against my collection.

So what do you want? Mr. Jones asked.

I leaned on his door frame.

I had no real reason except every reason. I had no real purpose except to tell him everything I noticed, to hear everything he noticed, and from both our noticings make some rules I could live by. Instead, I reached in my back pocket and pulled out the 50. Unfolded its black numbers, sharp and unmistakable, and flattened it out with my hand until it faced him. It in no way resembled any of his numbers. But he was my favorite math teacher. He was the owner of the hardware store.

I wanted somebody to see, and I picked him.

This, I said. I found this. Do you recognize this at all? Did you happen to lose a 50?

He gave a wry smile. From the marathon, he said. He reached out his long slim fingers to it, tracing the curves.

Do you even go all the way up to 50? I asked.

He kept his fingertips on the plastic, going around the o,

fingernail on a racetrack, slow. He let out a breath. I have up to 75, he said. Because I am a hopeful man. But I've never once worn 75, he said, I think I might die of pleasure. He sighed a bit. Can you see it? You've got to be pretty much on top of the world to be wearing 50.

You were 42 the other day, I said.

That was a marvelous day, he said. But besides that, the tops I've been in the last decade has been mid-30s. 32. Maybe 37, once.

I think I saw that, I said. 37

He looked at me, and his eyes grew tired, and seemed to know a lot about everything then. He smiled slightly. That 42 was a very good day, he said. Now that was a very very good day.

He fingered 15 around his neck.

Maybe the 50 fell out of your stack, I said, wanting to drag out the time.

I have no stack, he said. I use hangers.

Could you check? I asked. I would really appreciate that.

He leaned on the door frame himself. Mona Gray, he said, almost wistfully, as if just then remembering me.

Remember? I asked. I was the only kid who understood the numbers. Today you're 15. That's not too good but it's not miserable. It's your most common choice. Could you see if your 50 is missing?

He shrugged. Why don't you come on in, he said.

And with that, he opened his front door wide. He turned and went inside, leaving me at the door frame.

I just stood there for a second, and then, nervous, stepped into the dark wood-floored hallway, into the dark carpeted living room, which smelled strongly of wax and unlit pipes, unsmoked tobacco.

Most of the living room furniture was commonplace, with a

dusty green couch and ivory curtains half-drawn. I could see through the window into his backyard, and on the edge I made out the familiar shapes of my parents' shrubs.

But directly in the center of the living room, where most people had a coffee table, was a black pot that looked like a modest cauldron, bubbling up and dribbling over with wax. It stood upon hot coals, trapped in some kind of tray, and a huge silver ladle with a wooden handle hung off its edge. The floor underneath it was covered with newspaper, to catch the drippings as they boiled over. Also on the floor, surrounding the cauldron, were number cutouts, made of tin. Scattered loosely, out of order. It smelled like a crayon factory. A few already-done numbers were hardening on the fireplace: 7. 19.

Over that fireplace, strung along the walls, were hooks, but instead of holding paintings, they supported the old finished numbers, hanging there on their strings, in chronological order, bordering the house. There were spaces missing, for the missing numbers, more than even the collection I'd found. The numbers still hanging were all made of wax, with slight variations in color, and from where I was standing, I could see 6–28, winding through the walls of the room, back into the hallway where I lost sight of them. I put down the numbers I'd brought in a careful pile, and gravitated toward my age. Lifting it off the hook, I took it into my hands, and was holding it, my number of years alive, beige wax slightly warm in the afternoon sun, when Mr. Jones returned, holding up a string on which dangled a fresh wax 50.

Nope, he said. Look here.

I hung the 20 carefully back on its hook and nodded. His 50 was perfectly shaped, unsullied by wearings, which made me sad. I folded up the marathon square, hiding the number, and held it, fingers by now used to the slip of the material, the toxic slide.

He shrugged again and returned the 50 to whatever room it inhabited.

Then he came back and walked over to the cauldron. Using the long metal ladle, he dipped into the wax and poured a spoonful into the stencil mold for a new 15. The wax spilled out, smooth and heavy, rich as chocolate but thicker and drier, and with that particular warm candle smell. It settled in the 15 evenly and began to set. He leaned down, as if with a lit birthday candle, and gently blew.

Where'd you find the cauldron? I asked.

His face was focused and clear. Hardware store of course, he said, blowing.

He rotated the 15 in his hands, letting the liquid, already hardening, slide into the details of the mold, the hat on the 1, the tight angle at the top of the 5. I stood close to the wall, one hand on the nubby wallpaper. I didn't want to leave. I found the sight of him spilling warm wax into molds amazingly soothing. I felt, by far, the calmest I had all week.

Why'd you take off those other ones? I asked.

He picked up the ladle again.

Oh, he said, I suppose I'd had enough of them then. He smiled. And now I want them back, he said.

He checked on the 15. The wax was gelling, almost hard by now. Redipping the ladle, he put on a second layer, smooth and even.

I watched the wax roll around until it cooled and heavied, slowing. I was debating with myself whether or not it was rude for me to still stand there, staring, when Mr. Jones looked up from blowing on his brand-new 15, and did the thing it took him ten years to do.

So, he said. What did happen to your father anyway? he asked. The man has faded. And you, he said. You faded, too.

He carried the new 15 over to the fireplace and carefully set it aside. Then he leaned down and picked up another stencil, the infamous and powerful 42. I was distracted by that for a second when I realized what he'd just asked. My heart rose up.

What? I said, holding up my arm, peach, to the partial light filtering in through the curtains. Look, I said. I'm not faded.

You faded too, he repeated. Faded, faded, faded. I saw those track meets, he said. You were so good, that stride of yours.

What? I said again.

I cheered and cheered even though you'd turned into a little brat by then, he said.

I quit the team, I said.

I know, he said emphatically. He picked up the ladle again. You were taking the makeup test in math class and told me, he said. You were doing that odd thing with the pencil.

Wait, I said, you don't even remember who I am.

He sniffed at that. Dipping back into the cauldron, he poured another thin layer of hot wax into the shape of the 42. It crawled through the mold, taking on the angles of the 4, spinning down the hunchback of the 2.

Anyway, he continued, I enjoyed myself so much at the track meet that I went back, but you were gone by then. I found another star but she wasn't quite as good. Then I got pneumonia, that was a bad month. 6's and 7's.

That's right, I said. We had awful substitutes the whole time.

I leaned harder on that wallpaper. Mr. Jones turned his face to mine, eyes bright. He lifted the old 15 off his neck, broke the string off with his hands, and tossed it straight into the cauldron. It drifted on the waxy hot sea for a second, shoddy old 15, a faithful true life it had led, until it sank slow as a doomed ship into the beige depths. Jones watched it, we both did, then he turned around and walked to the number wall, took down 19, and slipped it over his head.

I like visitors, he said. This is good for me.

I shifted my weight on the wall.

So how come you never said anything, I asked. If you noticed all this stuff.

What do you mean? he asked.

I mean, there you were, saying how important it was to notice things. You noticed the pencil, I was grateful for that, I said. But how come you never said anything about this fading stuff?

But I did, he said, blowing on the 42.

I shook my head. What are you talking about? I asked. I even egged your garage one year because you said nothing to me about anything.

That was you? His eyebrows raised. I blanched slightly. My goodness, he said. That was really awful of you.

I know, I mumbled. Sorry about that.

He fiddled with the 19, supporting the bottom with his thumb, and redipped the ladle to give 42 its second coat.

Well, he continued, you must've egged me for saying something then. Because this is exactly what happened. I went to you some afternoon, you were playing on the lawn, and I said: Mona, you seem upset. And you said to me, and I'm certain of this, you said: Shut up Mr. Jones.

I did not say that, I said.

Well, he said, I am quite sure you did. I asked you if your father was okay and you said he was just fine and why was I even asking. You were a very snotty little kid.

I was a great math student, I said. I really said that?

Sure, he said. You were an excellent math student. The ladle brimmed with wax, and he stood there, poised. But you were a very snotty little kid, he repeated.

Hang on, I said, how come you remember all of this all at once? Five minutes ago you thought I was here to sell you cookies.

He scrunched up his lips, close to his nose, then lowered them. Didn't you buy the ax for your twentieth birthday? he said.

I had a sudden urge to melt down all his numbers all at once in that cauldron, dump every wall-hanging mood inside, then take off my clothes and step into it, a smooth wax glove, coating myself with every age, every mood, everything as available as skin.

You really asked that? I said.

He nodded. Sure did, he said. Then I stopped asking. His eyes were away, reviewing it all in his head. He poured the ladle down on the 42, second layer.

I don't remember any of that, I said.

So is he all right? Mr. Jones asked, his eyes returning to me.

The 50 was still tight in my hands, paper untouched by the new warmth in my palms.

He thinks he's about to die, I said quietly.

Mr. Jones nodded. I see, he said. He blew again on the 42, a gentle careful wind. The number settled and hardened. And you? he asked.

Sometimes I think I'm about to die, yeah, I said.

No no, Mr. Jones said. I meant do you think *he's* about to die?

I looked straight at him. He was looking straight at me. My palms were all over the 50, lifeline direct on those black fast numbers. Mr. Jones was waiting. The 42 was gelling. I opened my mouth, and the response that came out of it shocked me entirely.

No, I said. I don't.

26

The next day I walked over to Lisa's house, because I knew the address, because Elmer said it all the time now: 265 Ogden Place. No one was home, so I left a note in the mailbox saying I'd be coming by the school next week to pick up my things and some afternoon I'd like to take her to the park, or the movies, or the hospital, and that just because I was fired didn't mean she would never see me. I know where you live, I wrote. Inside the envelope I also put a leaf that I'd ripped into the shape of a 3, and wrote: $3 \times 3 = ?$ Love, Ms. Gray.

On Saturday, I spend the whole day cleaning the apartment. I make the kitchen floor so white it's a dentist's dream; I vacuum; I scrub the shower grout. I shine the kitchen faucet until I can see my eye on the nozzle. I fill the trash can with a bouquet of dirty paper towels from dusting. I throw out magazines. He shows up at eight. The apartment smells of detergent which reminds me of axes and he sits on the couch where I lied and fiddles with the pillow corners and says he saw Ann a few days ago. A mess of stitches up her leg, he says. She was bossing all the nurses around, he says, laughing. She's okay? I ask about five times. She's limping a bit for now, but she seems to be all right, he says. I keep nodding. I'm not sure where to put my relief plus I'm so nervous I can hardly look at him. He's wearing a T-shirt that says SCIENCE on it in block orange letters. His hair is messy. I think of Ann in her bed at home now, trays piled by her bedside, every different kind of pudding, spoons drying inside plastic cups. I get Benjamin a glass of water that he hasn't asked for, and he stands up to take it and I know I have to make the first move so I do it fast—he's swirling the water, clear liquid inside hard glass, it reminds me of the hospital, and I step in closer, halve the space, and I just spend some time with the inside of his elbows, the burn marks from the science class. He watches me closely. I don't kiss his mouth right away, I kiss instead his neck and the side of his cheek and the inside of his elbow.

We walk over to the couch and then we decide to walk over to the bedroom and our shoes are coming off and the magnets are charging up and I can feel the soap waiting for me in the bathroom, sitting there in its porcelain soap dish calling my name, Come on in Mona Gray, yoohoo Mona, get this over with. Come on in and visit. Come ruin everything. I'm holding his fingers, lightly, and I don't know if I can do this on my own. Our faces are close and I'm learning about his mouth again and his lips are warm and Ann is okay and the kiss keeps changing shape and size and speed and I'm going to try to foil this, I can just feel it, and the lights are off in the whole apartment and the bedroom is just shadows, curtains hanging, unmoving, and the bluish form of the bed. We stand over the bed and he sits down on the edge and I am straddling him, and our hips are starting to glue together, and I am in love with the way his elbow meets his forearm, the muscle on his shoulder, the hardness of his collarbone, the way he's made, so complete and simple, so mysterious and complicated, and I'm getting scared. I open my mouth to speak, tentatively, terrified, and I say it. I need to go to the bathroom, I say. Next door, the soap rears up in the soap dish, lathered, foaming, eager, ready. His hand is on my stomach. Come in here; come ruin it. He stops kissing me and looks straight at me and his teeth are white in the darkness. There is a long pause and I am waiting, and my hope is eighty airplanes, poised on the runway, ready for takeoff: please, please, please, please. And then he smiles. No, he says.

As soon as he says it my eyes fill up, just like that, the gratitude is that fast and that immediate, but I don't trust anything so we're kissing more and his lips are sweet as orange slices on a plate on a porch in the summer with weeping willow trees and larks, and then I ask him again, sure he'll get reasonable here; I say, in a more urgent voice: Hang on, I have to go to the bathroom. He is still looking at me, watching me, and says, no, voice stronger now, and I say, But I have to go, really, I mean it, and he shakes his head and says: No. Today I have decided to be your bathroom monitor and today I say no. The soap lather crawls over the edge of the porcelain and spills into the sink, somersaults of white. I was just kidding, I tell him, that thing I said the other day, I was just kidding, but he looks at me and shakes his head again. No. I grip his shoulders and his lips are drinking mine and then hands on my shirt and he's unbuttoning me and air moves into my blouse and I feel the skin on his back, how it falls into the spine, like waterfalls into a riverbed, my fingers boats traveling up the stream of his vertebrae and for a second I feel like I'm safe from myself. Panic lifts into kites. I ask him again. I need to go, I mumble, but now he just says, Come here Mona Gray, and leans back on the bed, takes me down with him.

When his shirt is off there's no part of him I find better than the burns up and down his arms and I am kissing them over and over. This is where he melts, this is his bathroom trip, and he says to me: You don't have to do that, it is ugly there, and I say: I think it's beautiful, and he doesn't believe me still and so I whisper how Danny brought in the severed arm to class as a 1 and the parents rioted but I thought it was wonderful, sealed in blue glass like that, the palm opened like a bud, and he starts laughing and laughing until his voice gets ragged and I can feel the room shift, the whole room is keeping us, and I ask him again because I can, because I am starting to have the smallest, most precious glimmer of trust; I say: I still have to go to the bathroom. His laughter is quieter now because I have been kissing each finger, each burn, each whorl, each cut, and he says: Too bad Mona Blue Green Gray because I am the bathroom monitor and you are not allowed to leave this bed. Lather drains into the sink, thinning. I make a move to leave but his hand clamps over my wrist and I say: I want to go NOW, but his hand is a brace and I slam against it. His fingers chafe my wrist. Pull harder. Pull. His hand is strong. I pull as hard as I can, throw the weight of my whole body against his hand, more, and I never get to do this, I never pull as hard as I can, I always pull less hard than I can just in case, but here I am straining, feet braced against the bed for leverage, and his hand is strong and wiry and I say: Let Me Go! and he is laughing at me and he says: You keep trying if you want but I will not let you go. I will not let you go.

My father was a track star in college and I was a track star in high school but I never ran against him, I never ran until I won, and that is the child's job, to have the one day where I run faster than my track-star father and the scepter gets passed and the trophy changes rooms. I wasn't fast enough at age nine; I was much faster at age sixteen, but by then he was grayed and quiet and gone. I have never really raced him and I never will race him; he can't race; he gets too tired and he once told me he doesn't like it if his heart beats so fast—that thumping, the insistence—I hate it, he said. So I stopped when he stopped. You faded, said Mr. Jones, blowing on his 42. Faded, faded, faded. You dropped off the number chart, he said. Now, the science teacher is right beside me, right here, fingers clamped on my wrist, saying: This is it? This is how hard you can pull? This is it? You're WEAK, he says to me and I start laughing, loud, and I am pulling against his hand as hard as I can and he's pulling back and the lamplight from outside the window is flickering over his skin like fire. I'm still laughing, barking, and I choke it out again: Bathroom, I say, but it's a joke now and he just says: Pee in the bed then bucko.

In the next room, the soap is a quiet dry stone. He uses both arms and brings me up on the bed, pulls me on top of him. Everything slows down. His skin is warm. The room is awake.

In high school, we lined up at the starting line together, eight of us side by side, coltish and muscled. Shoes like slippers. Stomachs full of wise breakfasts. Eyes clear, eye whites milky. When the gun went off, it always took me a millisecond to remember what was happening. Bam. Boom. Go. The others would get ahead, the numbers on their backs moving up and down, 5, 11, 98, 42. I'd watch them moving. 50, 20. 40, 10. My stride took three strides to catch, but then, like a machine engaging, it rolled forward: leg after leg after leg. The numbers floated ahead of me and they were like a beacon, a beckon, flat and hard, black and clean, and I'd pass them and the track would curve and I'd lean and push forward, past the air, past the noise, past the movement. Past everybody.

The clothes come off. His wristbones are sharp.

My father sat in the bleachers, wearing a hat against the sun. He always brought me a water afterward and I pretended I was happy to see him. I said, Thanks for coming Dad and Thanks for the water Dad and I talked and chatted and talked and kept talking so I wouldn't accidentally open my mouth and do the thing I felt which was to call him a quitter.

Benjamin's fingers move over me. He tells me something about my shoulders. I tell him something about his back. I can't leave the room. I'm not allowed to leave the room. We shift and roll over. I stop smiling.

Breathe in. The room gets darker. Hands.

In the locker room, I unlaced my shoes. I got a lot of congratulation hugs. The coach walked over, her lipstick stretched and wrinkled from beaming, and told me I beat my own record. She waited for me to react but I just pulled off my shoes one at a time and piled them into the steel-smelling locker. I don't want to beat my *own* record, I told her.

His hands are on my face and we're wrapped around each other then and it's slow and silent and intent, nothing fancy, nothing new; if people were watching in the movie theater they'd file out to the box office, demanding their money back, bored. What's going on with those two, they'd say, they are just taking their own sweet time, aren't they.

His thighs. The stream up his spine. The thin paper of his eyelid. The hair smell of his hair. The absurd asinine inane idiotic perfect simplicity of the fit.

On the clock, the red digital lines, wickedly bright, shuffle and restructure: 11:59; click: 12:00. Only the movement of three numbers at once makes me blink and notice: midnight. Tomorrow. Sunday. Which means it is my father's birthday. Which means he is 51 years old. And inside all the dizziness, Benjamin's eyes closed, mine open to darkness, the air in my chest thickening to a wheeze, warriors with weapons overtaking my body, distant movement getting closer, I think for a second that I am Joanna Stuart, the caboose of the family, taking off my clothes, melding skin with a boy in a Florida bed, and she thinks, as she pushes her hips down into his, I'm still here, she thinks, I have been here the whole time, haven't I, and the broom thought that finally sweeps me away is just that I am young. I am younger.

I am supposed to outlive them both.

27

The next afternoon, I spent an hour downtown at the bookstore picking out a book for my father. I considered something on skin disease and then another book on TV movies and something else on effective gardening but I kept returning to a big beautiful photo album of runners, black-and-white images, in the steel colors that make athletes gleam like statues. I carried it around the store for a while, bought it, and walked home with my arms around the wide cover. My body felt tired and calm. I'd sent the science teacher home in the morning, before noon, after we spent over an hour in bed talking about every kid in the school and I laughed so hard at his imitation of Danny O'Mazzi I had to go to the bathroom to pee and he followed me in, saying: You're still not allowed to go to the bathroom, and I twisted, laughing, said: This is for real, and he nodded and went to have some cereal. I peed, then washed my hands with shampoo. The soap was in the soap dish and looked, at that moment, the size of a piece of soap.

I wrapped my father's gift in tinfoil, put on a dress, and walked over. Knocked on their door. He opened right away—alive, alert— and hugged me. He was now 51, the most unmagical number of all. Happy birthday, I said. So nice to see you, he said. Everything seemed exactly the same as always, which made my heart hurt. I handed over the big square, which he received, smiling, then went to the living room, sat on the couch, and unpeeled it meticulously. How wonderful! he said when the cover was revealed. I nodded. Quiet. Will you look at these pictures, he cooed. He pored carefully over each page. He liked the active pictures the best—the one of five people jumping hurdles at the same second. The one of the woman arching through the air to break the tape and win. When he was done, he leaned over and kissed my forehead. Smart daughter, he muttered, proud.

My mother, looking beautiful in a slow burgundy dress, walked in, put a hand on the back of my neck, and said: 51! She kept laugh- ing about it. I can't believe you're 51, she said to my father. You look like you're about 75.

She kissed his check, long. My mother melted on birthdays.

We were going to dinner soon, at the fancier restaurant in town, and my father opened his other gifts and tried on various sweaters, most of which he found itchy. While my mother finished getting ready, he took me outside to the backyard and showed me the new *Shape of Health* he'd made early that morning while my mother was still sleeping; this one, he explained, had a slightly larger radius. I think the first was too small, he said, so I thought I'd try a bigger range. What do you think? he asked, eyes open and eager. You're the math teacher.

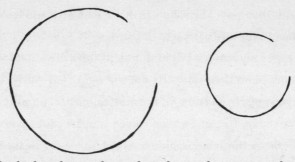

I looked at the two burned circles in the grass, each with the open mouth at one end.

You're good at circles, I said. Look how even they are. Did you make these freehand?

He nodded.

They're very even, I said.

He stepped inside first one, then the other. He smiled at me, welcoming. It seemed like he wouldn't mind now if I came closer, now that there were two, but I stayed on the uncircled grass, the grass that was just blades. He did a few stretches inside the larger circle, and then stepped out.

When it was time to go, we went out front to get in the car, and my mother muttered something about candles and ran back inside. Day was becoming night, and some new kid I didn't know was on his bicycle, out on the street, pedaling, back and forth, back and forth, tires rattling. The breeze was chilly, tree trunks cool to the touch.

I sat on the curb to wait, and my father walked over and sat down next to me. The kid biked by, focused the way kids on bikes are.

We sat side by side, my father and I. We sat alike, legs pushed out in front, feet crossed. He looked like he always looked. I was watching our legs, watching that kid on his bike, when, in the middle of this, of all people, the art teacher popped into my head. How whenever she laughed, she clamped a hand over her mouth. I laugh just like my mother, is what she usually said, in horror. Oh God, she said, I'm so terrified I'm going to be exactly like my mother.

I nodded when she said it, but I never really understood her. I didn't understand the big deal. Everyone said what she said, but it was the opposite that broke my heart.

This.

My father sat, feet out, on the curb, a walking half-century. A faded photograph. The pewter moons of his fingernails, the old black stems of his eyelashes, the distant circles around his pupils, the distant circles burned into the grass of the backyard. The gray, carefully creased pant-leg bulb of his knee.

I sat, feet out, on the curb, a walking fifth-of-a-century. But my dress had purple flowers all over it. I'd put it in the washing machine once on hot even though they said not to do that. I'd stuck a week's worth of newspaper in the dryer with it to see what the print might do. I drew all over it with pencil until it shimmered with lead but still. Still. The cloth was stubborn with lilacs and violets, held together by vines of rich greens and browns.

The kid went by on his bike again. He had a lot of freckles on his bare arms. I thought he might glance over, and notice; laugh and point out the difference between the two people sitting on the curb. But he just rode on by. I looked back and forth, from the purple to the gray, and waited for my father to tighten up. To accuse me of something. Treason. But he just said: You look lovely Mona. He sat on the curb and complimented my necklace. I told him happy fifty-first, and his cheeks darkened, a soft blush.

I'm sorry, I said, quietly, but I don't think I can keep you company anymore.

He just smiled. He just said: Mona. My wonderful child. My beautiful daughter. It's fine with me if you'd rather wait in the car.

28

Turned out Ann DiLanno's parents didn't die yet either. In fact, what happened was they won the state lottery. Ann's mother had a thing about 4's so she used 4, 14, 16, 24, 32, 44, and nailed the sterling combination. Ann got out of the hospital with those spider stitches climbing up her thigh, and on the second day she was back in her own bed, one day before her father turned 43, the family cashed in that winning lottery ticket for an even million dollars. They got their stuff together and moved out of town.

Ann returned to school for five minutes, the same day I was there, cleaning up the stuff I had left. The new math teacher had taken down my gallery of numbers, which were probably now poking out of garbage bins, fading 5's and 2's among banana peels and cartons of milk, and she was droning on by the chalkboard about the tens place. Two of the kids at the table were asleep.

I hadn't seen Ann since the accident. We ran into each other in the front room, among all the coats and lunch boxes. Kids milled about, waiting for recess to begin.

I stood over her, holding a box full of workbooks. Ann, I said. I am so, so sorry.

She tossed her hair, loose from her ponytail, straight brown and practical. She was wearing a little purple mink coat, and holding up a 3 made of gold that she wore on a gold chain around her neck.

I have a real one now, she said. It's gold. $3 + 3 = 6$. $3 - 3 = 0$.

Hey, said John Beeze. Can I see the stitches?

Ann twirled the 3 around her index finger.

This is what I wanted to show you all, she said. I'm going to take it with me, my gold 3. I liked your class Ms. Gray, she said to me. She looked at everyone milling around. I was glad to know y'all, she said.

They were moving to Texas. She'd already morphed into a Texan, before she'd ever even left town.

Grab a brochure on your way out, I said.

She leaned against the table. She didn't seem to be limping much. She looked around the room, forehead sweating from the mink coat, and a couple of the younger kids were standing near her arm, petting it. She was a celebrity at school now for multiple reasons: wounded Ann, wealthy Ann. On impulse, she lifted her skirt and showed the little kids her spidery stitches, so black and so many they made my heart drop, the straight-line thick scar that lovers would touch later to identify their Ann in the darkness. The smaller kids shrieked and shivered and stared.

Her thigh the longest memory of Numbers and Materials, ready to announce rainy weather, to outlive both me and the school.

Lisa walked over from another room to look at the stitches. She had her own in a row on her forehead. There was some mutual admiration and then Ann nudged Lisa and fumbled in her pocket, handing over a box of crayons, all beige—every shade, from ivory to tan.

I hope your mom gets better, Ann said.

Lisa took the crayons and nodded. Have fun in Texas, she said.

She paused for a minute, and then ripped out a few ratty hairs from her head.

Here, she said. Here's some hair to remember me by.

Ann folded it into her mink pocket, pleased.

Lisa poked me. I bent down. Ms. Gray, she whispered into my ear, there is nothing to draw that's beige.

Ducks? I whispered back.

She rolled her eyes and walked away. Later that day, as I was leaving, I found the crayons stuffed in my jacket pocket along with a folded drawing of a duck done in rich metallic greens and blues.

I am a rich kid now, Ann declared right before she left, looking a little nervous.

I wanted to give her a hug but wasn't sure it was allowed. She leaned into me awkwardly. I squeezed her shoulder, hard.

Just remember you are good at math, I said.

After Ann left, I brought my box of supplies to my apartment and put them under the bed for some other day. Then I went back to the school, and skulked outside until Lisa was done. I saw Danny in between classes and he smiled at me. Hello Ms. Gray, he said, the most polite I'd ever seen him. He had the clear eyeballs of a good milk drinker, a future star quarterback. I waved once from the front doorway to Benjamin, who was busily combing his hair and dumping salt and pepper into a bowl full of water to prep for a demonstration about magnetics. He said he'd come by later. I told him I was taking Lisa to the movies and then the hospital, and hopefully he could meet us after. BANK ROBBERY! had finally switched, and now they were playing a musical about New York City. Lisa had liked my 3 note and I'd found one in my mailbox two days later, with twigs taped together in the shapes of a 5 and a 6, and a piece of paper that said Okay.

When she was all done with her classes, Lisa put on her backpack, took my hand, and we started over toward the park. I told her that the stitches on her forehead made her look like addition: $+++++$, and she smiled. Plus plus plus, she said. I want to start on division now, she said.

We walked past the Stuarts' old house. Joanna off swimming somewhere. We walked by Mrs. Finch's old house. We walked by my parents' house. We walked by Mr. Jones's house. He was out watering his lawn, wearing a 20. I waved. How are you doing Mona? he asked. Pretty good, I called, and you? He's 20, announced Lisa. That's right, said Mr. Jones, winking. I squeezed Lisa's hand. Will the store be open later? I asked, and he said: Sure thing, and Lisa said: I didn't sleep well last night. So I'm about 11 today. Mr. Jones nodded firmly, and my heart brimmed with both of them.

We reached downtown, and I bought our tickets at the box office. Lisa suggested we sit in the park, since there was an hour or so before the movie started. It was about three-thirty and the sky was a nice easy blue. I gave her a few dollars to buy us ice cream and she went across the street while I looked at the ducks moving around on the dirt—the electric green of the mallard's neck, the egg brown feathers of his lady.

Lisa returned with two cones: a chocolate for me, a purplish one for herself.

What's yours? I asked. Chocolate raspberry?

It's raisin, she said, sitting back down next to me.

I took a lick of mine. It swept a line of chocolate onto the roof of my mouth.

Raisin? I said. They have raisin-flavored ice cream?

She counted the change into my hand. I threw it in the duck pond. Yes, she said. She blew some air out her mouth and said she was mad at Elmer because he always drew the same house picture and never anything else.

Raisin, I said, still taking that in.

We settled into the bench and watched the woman walk her scraggly dog and the man with the briefcase go into the candy shop.

Lisa was mostly quiet. She had a new tic, touching the stitches on her forehead back and forth, like a xylophone. She was barely eating her raisin ice cream. One short lick at a time. And Lisa was not a slow eater. Poor raisin, she sang, bringing it up to her mouth and then holding it out in front of her like it smelled bad; no one ever buys you, she said. Do you like raisin? I asked. No, she said, but I do like raisin-bran cereal. I laughed at her. I don't want raisin ice cream to go out of business, she added, looking a little annoyed at me. I gave her another two dollars and told her to go back and get what she really wanted. She came back in a few minutes with a blob of chocolate fudge for herself. She still gripped the raisin in her left hand. The chocolate disappeared in a few minutes and the raisin drooled a line of dark purple down her wrist.

She held the cone tight.

You want? she offered.

I shook my head. No thanks. I've never been a big raisin fan, I said, even in its regular form.

It's not bad, she said. She took another lick. She'd barely made a dent. It's good, she said.

You can throw it out, I told her, it's fine with me. You don't have to be polite, I don't mind.

I was squinting at the new brochures facing out of the tourist-office window when I said that, and not at Lisa, and so when I turned back a minute or so later, I was surprised to see her eyes had filled and were spilling over, glittering with water. She spent a few minutes wiping her face.

Oh Lisa, I said, what is it? I put a hand on her head. She cried for a little while, tears racing lines down her cheeks. After a few minutes, she spoke up. You can't throw out raisin ice cream, she said.

By now, the cone was melting in on itself, gloppy globules of purple-brown. Lisa kept sniffing. A green duck walked by. Across town, Ann's family was packing up their boxes into big moving vans. The hospital loomed over the trees, a vase of toothless daisies.

We still had a good half hour until the movie started.

What do you want to do? I asked. We could go to the drugstore, I said. She shook her head. We could go to the candy shop, I said. She shrugged. She was still clutching that ice cream cone.

We could do some long division, I said.

Do you know any math stories? she asked.

She tucked up her legs beneath her on the bench, and licked a little ice cream off her wrist.

Math stories? I said.

She nodded, yawning. She had raisin all over her hands now.

I leaned back and thought for a second, looking at the archway

of trees around us. My mother's tourist office. The watery blue of
the sky. The hardware store, closed.

I knocked on the bench. She knocked back, staring up at me,
eyes vivid and livid and limpid.

I know a math story, I said then.

29

Lisa balanced the raisin ice cream cone on the bench. She stretched out into a good listening position, resting her head on my leg. I put a hand down and smoothed the bumpy lumps of her hair.

Okay, I said slowly.

She looked up at me, blinking, expectant.

A couple of ducks floated by on the duck pond, tucked into green and brown ovals. My throat clogged up.

And I backed out.

It was a pond of addition frogs, I said suddenly. There were twelve frogs in one pond and fourteen in another. How many frogs were there total?

I didn't look down at Lisa.

She gave a gentle hiccup in my lap.

That's the math story? she muttered. That's not a story. Twenty-six.

She pulled a scrap off her raisin cone and threw it into the pond where it floated along, uneaten. Then she turned on her side, curling her body up on the bench. I would be meeting her mother after the movie. We had a plan to go buy a Gravlaki address at the hardware store and bring it up to Mrs. Venus's unnumbered room and present it to her. It's important to have a number on your door so Elmer can know where you live. Lisa was excited about it. She said we could all eat hospital dinner together and maybe if I was lucky she would show me how to skid down the hallway in my socks.

Don't you know any other stories? she asked, on my lap. Better ones?

I moved my hand over her hair, slow. Through the trees, a tiny albino eyebrow of moon waxed high and far on the blue.

Lisa licked chocolate off her fingertips.

Okay, I said.

She stuck her wrist in her mouth, licking off more ice cream, waiting.

Here's a story I made up for you, I said.

Put a 3 in it, she mumbled.

I rested my hand on her forehead.

And a pirate, she said. I like pirates.

Okay, I said. It starts with a kingdom, I said.

I like kingdoms too, Lisa garbled, mouth full of wrist.

I kept my voice low. It was hard to talk through the swell in my throat.

There was once a kingdom, I began, of pirates.

This pirate kingdom had discovered the gift for eternal life, I said. That means no one ever died there, so there were no cemeteries, and no obituaries. The eye patch was just a fashionable accessory. No one walked the plank, except to go swimming. Wars weren't tragic. Flags were not revered. There were no glass hospitals and red wigs and I.V.'s; there weren't any bad eye cells or casseroles. Cancer was not a big deal.

Lisa murmured approval, running damp fingers over her stitches. I stroked the rolls and waves of her hair.

But there was a big problem in this pirate kingdom, I said. It was way too crowded. Food was running out, and water was at an all-time low, and so the king pirate, who was also known throughout the land as a great mathematician, decided to issue a decree. He said: "I have done the math and the truth is clear. According to the ratio of birth to death, factoring in the amount of oxygen needed per person, using exponents and dividing by three, one pirate in each household must die." He said, "Come to the town square and bring your volunteer, or else please leave."

But none of the other towns knew the secret to eternal life.

I looked at the head on my leg. Are you okay so far? I asked. Lisa nodded, eyes closed, listening. I put my other hand, soft, on the wood of the park bench.

So on the chosen day, I said, keeping my voice low, the entire town congregated at the town square, where the skull-and-crossbones flag was flying for the first time in years. The executioner, wearing a big black pirate hat with a red carnation in the brim, rested a hand gently on the gallows. The king pirate held a huge piece of scroll covered with numbers. "Now," the king boomed, "it is time, as a town, for us to make more by making less." There was a little bit of scattered cheering. He bowed to the families, who each tearfully offered forward their special chosen volunteer, and the king checked each person off his list. All was settled and ready to go except for one family of pirates. This family said they couldn't decide. First the mother had offered to die, but no one liked that, and then the father, and then the sister, brother, baby pirate. But no one was happy with any of the options. The mother announced: "We'll all die." But the town didn't like that, and frankly, neither did the rest of the family.

So the father stepped forward and said, "Why don't we offer forward a piece of each of us? I'll cut off my nose, my wife will cut off her arm, my daughter can cut off her ear, my son his foot."

I whispered it into the air. So quiet only we could hear. Lisa was resting on my leg, sucking on her wrist, her breathing steady and calm. The wave rose, thick, inside my throat, and I pressed my palm on the bench. Listen: I tell the wood—listen to what I'm doing here. Mark this down. Notice.

The king pirate, I whispered, the great mathematician, said it wouldn't be quite as effective as the removal of an entire person, but he was intrigued by the concept of fractions and was willing to consider the idea of a group effort.

The mother nodded eagerly, and the father nodded nobly, and the brother held out his foot, wanting to get it over with as fast as possible.

But the daughter shook her head and stepped forward.

"In the next town over," she said, "I've heard they have a fish pond. Can't we just leave and go there?"

"But daughter," said the mother, father, brother, and baby. "If we leave, we'll all die eventually. This town is special, this town is the only town that knows the secret to eternal life. Only one pirate has to die to save the rest of us from disease and death *forever*."

The daughter listened. She nodded. But she kept talking. "But I don't want to cut off my ear," she said. "I want to be able to hear things. I want to see my mother use her hands. I'd like to see my father with a nose. I want to see my brother with shoes on. I hate hooks," she said.

"But daughter," said the mother, father, brother, and baby. "Once you die, you won't get to hear or walk or use your hands or comb your hair at all."

All the kingdom was waiting for her answer. Some of the volunteer-death people shivered.

The daughter stared in the distance. There were ants walking in a row on the ground. They made a perfect line.

"I'm leaving," she said. "Anyone else want to come?"

The entire town leaned back. There was a wave of surprised murmurs.

The mother shook out her sacrificial arm. "Well," she said. "I suppose we can rob ships anywhere."

The father seemed annoyed. "I like eternal life," he said.

The daughter hugged everyone and then began walking away, past the gallows, past the flag, past the volunteers, over toward the yellow rolling hills. The executioner pirate looked rejected. The king rapidly worked equations on his paper, brow crumpled with confusion. After a minute, a couple of the volunteer-death people began following her, until a crowd of about fifteen trailed her path. The brother joined them. The mother said she'd try to meet them there soon with the baby pirate, but she wanted to pack first. The father kept shrugging.

"I don't know about this," he said.

From a long distance, the daughter turned around and waved. "Bye," she yelled. "I'll be next town over."

The father and mother waved back, and for a moment all you could see were their three hands in the air, a family, palms at each other, waving in the afternoon light like sunflowers. The hills were bright and yellow. The daughter's fingers stayed up, still moving, and the mother's fingers waved back and the father's fingers waved back and for a while all their hands were exactly the same size, exactly the same shape, until the daughter's grew smaller and smaller, and when the hill dipped down, it was gone and so was she. The mother put down her arm. The father kept waving and waving, but his hand was alone in the air now. The king was still trying to make sense of it all, pencil flying across paper. A couple of townspeople wanted to watch her longer, so they scrambled on top of the gallows to gain height. Sure enough, they immediately spied her blue-clad back again, moving forward, down the hillside, with the small troop of people trailing behind her. The viewers watched on their tiptoes, twenty feet high, as the departing group walked straight into death, and they watched as long as they could, her knees, her waist, her shoulders, the top of her head, but in minutes the path had sloped down again and even the people on the gallows could see nothing more than an empty yellow hill rolling out in front of them like a carpet of sunlit water.

Acknowledgments

I am very thankful for the support and sustenance of many, and in particular, this team of people who fill and refill the glasses of faith and patience. I feel so grateful for: invigorating discussions with ever-supportive Meri Trust-the-Process and David Teacher-of-Metaphors Bender; the crucial forward hurtle encouragement of Suzanne Bender, and Karen Bender who inspires; the wonderful wisdom and push of Jeanne Burns Leary; the excellent readings of Geoffrey Wolff, Michelle Latiolais, and Phil Hay. I'm ridiculously indebted to the consistent rigor and investment of: superconnected reader and friend Miranda Hoffman, structure king Glen Gold, the line-editing brilliance and support system of Alice Sebold, and thematic tsar of synthesis and much more, Teal Minton. Also big thanks for the warmth and smarts of my agent Henry Dunow and the insight and vigor of my terrific editor Bill Thomas.

AIMEE BENDER

The Particular Sadness of Lemon Cake

THE NEW YORK TIMES BESTSELLER

'A book with such beautiful writing that sometimes
I have to stop and taste a sentence a second time'
JODI PICOULT

On the eve of her ninth birthday, Rose Edelstein bites into her mother's homemade lemon-chocolate cake and discovers she has a magical gift: she can taste her mother's emotions in the slice. All at once her cheerful, can-do mother tastes of despair and desperation. Suddenly, and for the rest of her life, food becomes perilous. Anything can be revealed at any meal.

Rose's gift forces her to confront the truth behind her family's emotions - her mother's sadness, her father's detachment and her brother's clash with the world. But as Rose grows up, she learns that there are some secrets even her taste buds cannot discern.

The Particular Sadness of Lemon Cake is about the pain of loving those whom you know too much about, and the secrets that exist within every family. At once profound, funny, wise and sad, this is a novel to savour.

'Intense, strange and incredibly moving, it captures the
magic and romance of the unknown'
ELLE